MOUNTAIN MAN VS. GRIZZLY

GENE TURNEY

D1113417

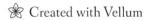

This novel, as are all my novels and everything I do, is dedicated to Cheryl, my children, grandchildren, nieces, nephews, cousin Pat, and other in-laws and outlaws and many friends' encouragement. Without the faith and encouragement of so many, this book would not exist. With great appreciation, I acknowledge the people who have provided invaluable assistance to the development of this particular novel.

FOREWORD

Boots McCray stumbles on the bodies of two trappers that he knew. They had both been mauled by a bear. Men make mistakes in the mountains, and Boots thought that is what had happened to his two friends. He found out a man-killer was roaming the mountain.

1

"There is not much going on around here. I think it is time for me to go on a hunt."

Boots McCray had all he could stand of the cold winter months. Signs of spring had put a new step in his walk. Boots had never been able to sit around without keeping his hands busy. He had the outlook of an eternal optimist. He always looked forward and he had a happy attitude. His wife Migisi told him that he smiled too much and it made her think he had some sort of medical problem.

The cave where Boots and his family lived in the Rocky Mountains served his family well. He and Migisi had raised a son and daughter. Those two had moved on to start their families. Both were living in the Cheyenne village where Migisi's father served as chief.

"You are welcome to come with me and hunt. Some days I think you are the better hunter," Boots said.

"You know I am the best hunter. I take one try and I never miss. You seem to think those bullets will fall from the sky the way you use them all. When you no longer have them, we must travel for days to get more. I use my bow and arrow. I can always make arrows without having to travel for days. My way is the right way."

Migisi had spent the winter months crafting four bows and quivers of arrows. She handed Boots a longbow and a short one. "When we walk, you take the longbow. When we ride, we will need the short one. I will teach you my ways. You will learn, and we will be happy,"

Boots had lived many years in the mountains. He knew well enough the way Migisi hunted would turn out to be successful, but he felt it necessary to let her know that he had been a good provider.

"I do not see that we have missed very many meals together. We do not go to bed hungry, and we have a plentiful supply of food. I want to learn your hunting, and I will take the longbow because we are going to leave our horses and burro. We will walk."

This hunting trip marked the first time Boots and Migisi would spend time foraging for game since they started their family. While they left the larder full at the cave, both were ready to get into the forest and find wildlife. The winter had been one of the most severe in recent years. Watching from the porch of the cave, they could see some snow rabbits scurrying along the edge of a park. The rabbits marked the only sign of life outside the cave where Boots and Migisi made their home.

Migisi had decided this would be her hunting trip and if Boots wanted to come along he could. She remembered his invitation to her to go hunting, but since that invitation had been issued, Migisi had taken charge.

"Your pack is heavy. Look at my pack. It is easy to carry because I leave my home in the cave. I think you have everything from the cave in your pack," Migisi chided Boots.

"My pack is heavy because I have to carry all of the supplies that you cannot put in your small pack. If we left my pack behind, we would have to come home in just a few days. I packed so we could stay out for as long as we want," Boots struggled with the sled that he pulled. The sled had been loaded with a few essentials, but he brought it mainly to haul the products of their hunt.

The bantering between Boots and Migisi continued as the two worked their way through the heavy snow. While early signs of spring had brought them from their cave, the snowmelt had yet to occur. Both wore heavy buckskin clothes and they each had a grizzly robe for warmth. Boots had fashioned new snowshoes for both and the shoes helped to trudge through the drifts.

"It has been a long time since we have been able to hunt

together," Boots huffed out his words as his breath became short in the effort to navigate through the snow.

Migisi and Boots met many years ago at the rendezvous for fur trappers. They were drawn to each other during the time spent at the rendezvous and eventually, they decided to set out for a life together.

Boots did not know that Migisi was the daughter of a Cheyenne chief. He suffered a severe beating when the braves caught up with the eloping couple. Eventually, the chief relented to allow them to marry. Boots carried a scar above his left eye that had been put there by Migisi's brother Red Feather. When Migisi looked at Boots, she saw the scar and remembered all the pair went through so they could be together.

2

They made only a few miles during their first day out. Both were winded and tired.

"We must stop and rest. I will find us a camping spot," Boots headed toward what looked like the edge of the forest with a park on the outside. He found a place where he and his son had camped while on a hunting trip years ago.

A tarp stretched from four small trees to give the camp cover from rain and the snow that fell from tree branches when a breeze made its way through. Because of the tree cover, the ground had a small amount of snow. Migisi made short work of clearing the snow and saving some of it for water. Once the ground had been cleared, Boots rolled out another tarp where they could put bedding and the supplies. Migisi made a small fire near the edge of the overhead tarp.

The smoke left the fire and slipped out the edge of the tarp. The two hunters sat with their legs crossed warming their hands at the fire.

"You have done well with this place. We can make this place our spot while we hunt," Migisi surveyed the forest and the park.

"I think I see a little stream in that park. If there is water there, we will find plenty to take home," Migisi smiled at Boots. "I am glad you left your bullets and gun behind. The noise from the gun scares everything away, and they take days to come back. When we hunt with arrows, we do not make a big noise."

Boots thought about the pack he had put together. That pack contained his two pistols and plenty of bullets for each.

He had wrapped the guns and ammunition in beaver pelts and Migisi did not see him put them in the pack. He wanted the guns, just in case something came up that he could not handle with a bow and arrow. While Migisi had been very encouraging when he practiced with the bow, Boots felt he could not be very efficient.

Migisi and Boots stayed in camp for two days getting settled and hoping for a little warmer weather to set in.

"We may have left our cave early, Migisi. I had become nervous about getting out and hunting, so I thought spring weather would be close. It feels colder now than when we left."

"I have been watching, and the weather will warm very

soon. The snow has not started to melt, but I feel signs in the wind. We are in a good place to start our hunting. We must find our places to hide so that we can have the advantage. I will look in the morning. I will go toward that park and you go the other direction."

Migisi pointed toward the east. Boots knew of a park in that direction, but he had not explored the area west of the camp.

They enjoyed the silence the forest brought as they finished their evening meal. Migisi felt grateful that Boots had brought extra supplies such as the two tarps that helped make the camp more comfortable. As they settled in for the night, buffalo robes were pulled up to their chins and the fire warmed their feet. Winter still made its presence known with the cold temperatures.

Boots woke with the noise of a pan being knocked against a rock. Water had been left in the pan from the last meal, and a thick layer of ice had formed. Migisi knocked most of the ice out of the pan and she turned her attention to getting the fire restarted.

As she moved around the camp, Boots noticed Migisi's breath forming a small fog as she breathed against the cold air. He quickly got to his feet to help with the preparations for the day. He gathered small pieces of wood for the fire and Migisi nodded her approval when he put an armload on the ground.

"We make a small fire and stay warm. When we make a

small fire, you do not have to go far to gather the wood. A big fire will use up all of the wood you could carry and then you would have to go far to get more. We will stay warm with this fire," Migisi grinned at Boots as she put some venison in the pan to cook. After a few minutes, the aroma of cooking meat permeated the forest.

After breakfast, Boots and Migisi set out on their scouting missions to explore possible hunting areas. Boots headed west, while Migisi headed east. Boots knew well enough that Migisi would find the best hunting because he and his son had hunted the area where she planned to scout.

Boots began to recall the blizzards and heavy snowfall that hit during the winter. Deep snowdrifts slowed him as he tried to find a track to get to a meadow or park. He found a shallow stream that had frozen so he walked on the ice for a long way. The ice did not show any signs of weakness, and Boots knew the stream would not provide fresh water for those trying to live through the winter.

Even so, he took care to stay close to the stream as he continued his search. Occasionally Boots would see what appeared to be a promising area. He would climb through a heavy snowdrift only to find fields of snow so smooth it seemed someone had cleaned away any signs of animal life.

After stopping for a noon meal, Boots started his trek back to the camp. He kept his hopes up for Migisi to find some good hunting ground because his trip to the west produced only hard labor and no hunting opportunities.

After a couple of hours walk, Migisi began to find signs of life as she scouted east of the camp. The east side of the Rocky Mountains seemed to have a warmer temperature. Snow had thinned to the point the snowshoes were no longer necessary. Migisi laced them together and tied them to the pack that she carried on her back. She stopped for a few minutes to rest and eat some jerky. She had found many tracks in the snow left by deer and antelope. She had been surprised when she discovered a moose roamed in the area. She sat under a large pine tree and she leaned back against the trunk of the tree. Her pack lay on the ground by her right side. Migisi closed her eyes for a brief respite and her sense of hearing picked up a noise a distance away. Something crashed through the brush, and Migisi could hear grunting. She stood and put her pack on her back, and she intuitively decided to get up in the tree so she would be able to see the source of the noise.

The pine tree must have been sixty to seventy feet tall. Migisi found the climb an easy one and she decided to stop when she found a suitable spot about twenty feet from the forest floor.

She stood on a hefty branch and looked to the south. She saw a black bear ambling along with three cubs following. The bear stopped at a stream and stood up. With a strong force, the bear slammed the front paws into the stream to break the ice. The black bear repeated the maneuver several times until clear water ran over the top of the broken ice. The three cubs were quick to the water.

"The mother bear is taking care of the little ones," Migisi thought. When she studied the mother bear, she could see the effects of a long winter. The big black bear looked almost skin and bones. The three cubs appeared to be in much better shape, and they played with energy. Migisi knew the mother bear is on the hunt for food.

After watching the cubs frolic in the stream, the mother bear started to move up the mountain in the direction where Migisi hid in the tree. Migisi had no fear of the bear because she had her bow and arrows, plus she had managed to be well hidden up in the pine tree. Migisi had no desire to try to kill the mother bear and leave the three cubs to fend for themselves.

"How soft-hearted I have become," thought Migisi. "not too long ago, I would be happy to take the mother bear and the three cubs. Now, I think I will leave them to go their way."

The mother black bear decided the way would be a straight line to the big pine tree where Migisi had her perch. The three cubs romped along with their mother as she ambled from side to side toward the tree.

"Has she picked up my smell," Migisi wondered. "I made no effort to hide anything because I thought the bears would still be in hibernation."

The bear stopped at the spot where Migisi had removed the snowshoes. She had to sit on the ground and she left impressions in the snow. The bear seemed to be a little confused by the discovery, but soon, she started sniffing and stirring up the snow, following Migisi's tracks to the big pine.

Migisi started thinking about a defensive strategy should the bear discover her presence in the tree. She did not want to kill the mother bear, she wanted the bear to continue with her cubs. She unstrapped the snowshoes to get access to her bow and quiver of arrows. If need be, she had plenty to take down the bear and the three cubs.

One of the cubs found where Migisi had rested against the tree trunk and tried to climb the tree. The cub had not aged enough to have strong claws to climb, however. Mother bear sniffed Migisi's scent at the base of the tree and wrapped her arms around the tree and used her sharp claws to dig into the soft trunk. The black bear pulled herself up with her arms and she brought her feet up to help. Fueled by the need to have something to eat, the bear started to scamper up the tree.

When the bear managed to get about halfway to Migisi's perch, Migisi stood by balancing on the big branch. She spread her arms out wide and yelled at the big bear.

"I am too big for you. I can fly like an eagle. You go away," Migisi kept repeating her words. The black bear stopped climbing and after a few minutes, she began to use her hind feet claws to ease back to the ground. Once on the ground, the black bear stood on her hind legs and let out a vicious bellar.

The cubs looked at their mother realizing they had never seen her act in such a way. All three scampered to a nearby tree where they occupied themselves with play. Undaunted by the big figure in the tree, mother bear sat on her haunches and looked up to find Migisi standing all of her five-foot frame trying to look larger than life.

Occasionally, the black bear would make an effort to climb the tree, only to be met with loud yelling from Migisi. Tiring from the continued effort from the bear, Migisi threw one of her snowshoes. The second the snowshoe left her hand, Migisi realized that had not been a good idea. The snowshoe bounced after hitting the bear in the head and it fell to the ground. The bear seemed as though she never felt a thing from the snowshoe, however, the bear worked her way back down the tree trunk.

The afternoon hours wore on. Mother black bear and the three cubs were content to wait until their meal climbed down from the tree limb. Migisi had no thought of leaving her perch. Darkness soon set in with four bears resting against the trunk of a huge pine tree, with Migisi twenty feet above them. She had sat in the fork of the limb and trunk eating a meal of jerky and biscuits. She had plenty of water, and Migisi had decided she would stay in the tree until the bear moved on. She looped a rope around the tree trunk and tied it around her waist as a safety measure should she fall asleep. The rope would keep her from falling on the bear.

Boots had managed to make his way back to camp to find Migisi still scouting. He began to get concerned when dark set in, and he decided he would set out early in the morning to find her.

3

Boots lay awake all night with worry about Migisi, thinking something terrible had happened to her. When morning broke, he picked up Migisi's trail.

Migisi did not rest easy during the night. Being tied to a tree twenty feet off the ground with bears surrounding the tree trunk tended to put one on edge. She had decided on a plan of action. Knowing the mother bear would be angry if something injured one of her cubs, Migisi thought she would wound one of them and see if the cub would run away, and she hoped the mother bear would follow to care for her young.

Migisi picked out a cub that lay on its belly on a deadfall log. She drew an arrow and sent it sailing toward the back leg of the cub. The arrow took a small slice in the leg of the cub, enough so the little bear would feel the injury, but the wound would certainly heal.

The cub shrieked when the arrow struck and he fell off the log. The arrow stuck deep into the log and a tuft of hair from the leg of the bear stuck out around the arrow. Migisi thought she may have been conservative in her aim and the arrow only pulled hair from the leg. She soon saw a trickle of blood in the snow.

Mother bear left her spot to investigate the problem with her cub. The cub had started to move down the mountain in the direction of the stream where the three had played. The black bear and the other two cubs were following the wounded cub.

Migisi breathed a sigh of relief. The bear family had left, but she dared not leave her perch until she could determine they would not return. She hoped they had lost interest in her.

Boots kept doggedly on the trail left by Migisi. He reached the spot where she had removed her snowshoes. He stopped and removed the snowshoes he wore and continued on the trail. He soon crossed tracks left by the bear family. He could tell three cubs followed a big bear. He was surprised to see bear tracks this early in spring, however, he thought maybe the bear came from down the mountain where spring would likely show up sooner.

Bear tracks crossed Migisi's tracks several times and Boots began to realize the bear had been on the hunt, and Migisi would likely be the target. Migisi had been raised in the Cheyenne village and she knew the land and she knew how to protect herself. Boots hoped that she would have an opportunity to mount a defense because the tracks looked as though the bear followed Migisi and a surprise attack from behind could be deadly. The long months in hibernation made for extreme hunger for the bear and they would be ravenous when they woke. Not only that, but this bear had three baby cubs to care for. This did not look like a good situation.

The forest had grown quiet and Migisi contemplated making her away to the ground and getting back to the camp. The bear had lost interest in her and had moved out of the area. She untied the rope that kept her from falling out of the tree and she stood on the sturdy limb to scan the forest for any sign of the bear. She caught a glimpse of movement. Something or somebody moved from one tree trunk to another as they approached her location.

Boots saw small dots of red blood in the snow. He could see the dots left a trail and he decided to follow. He had to decide to go left up the mountain, or right which would lead him down the mountain. He knew Migisi did not go down the mountain, but he could not tell if the blood dots belonged to her or something else. Boots became anxious for Migisi's well-being. He could hear his heart beating in his chest as he thought the worst had happened to her. He did recognize the bear tracks around the blood dots, and the tracks led down the mountain.

Boots kept following the tracks and the traces of blood. He came to a log where he saw an arrow had stuck in the wood. When he leaned down to inspect the arrow point, he noticed the tuft of hair from the cub. He also recognized the arrow and arrow point as being one that belonged to Migisi. He bent over the log with his face close to the arrow when he heard a whoosh and a thud. He felt the vibrations caused by the impact of an arrow striking the log. Boots fell back on the side of the log that would give him protection from another arrow.

He could see the shaft of both arrows and he knew those arrows belonged to Migisi. Boots lay as flat on the ground as the rocky terrain and snow would allow. His mind racked with confusion and he realized he had been holding his breath. When he exhaled and started breathing again, Boots thought he heard laughter and the laughter sounded like the laughter he heard from Migisi.

Not knowing who had fired those arrows, Boots decided to show a flag of truce. He tied a piece of cloth to one of the arrows from his quiver and waved the flag of surrender over the top of the log.

The laughter became louder as an arrow ripped through the flag.

"You must come out from your hiding place so that I can see you," Migisi yelled from her perch in the tree.

"I am staying right here until you tell me you will not shoot me full of arrows," Boots yelled back.

"Then you stay where you are," Migisi yelled, as she let another arrow fly just over the top of the log. The arrow plowed into the snow barely missing Boots.

Migisi shimmied down the tree trunk, walked over to the log, and leaned over to look into the face of her husband.

"I am happy to see you, husband," Migisi grinned at Boots. He was shocked and relieved to see Migisi. His mind had conjured the worst happening to her, but, yet here she was smiling down at him while he lay on the ground near the trunk of the tree.

"Your welcoming sure told me otherwise. You almost got me with those arrows, and you ripped up my flag."

"What is the idea of waving that thing in the air. I thought you put up a target for me to hit and I believe I did have a good aim."

"Migisi, that piece of cloth I waved in the air showed that I gave up, I quit, I surrendered to you," exclaimed Boots.

"Oh, I did not know. But, I wanted you to look up in the trees where I had hidden. You did not look, you started hiding."

Boots pulled Migisi down on top of him.

"Are you hurt? I followed a trail of blood to this log."

Migisi sat up on her knees.

"I am not hurt. That blood is from a cub that I had to shoot to get the bears to leave,"

Migisi went on to tell Boots of the encounter with the black bear and three cubs. She had been a strong woman as long as Boots had known her. While she related her story, Boots appreciated her strength and courage.

While Migisi retrieved her three arrows, Boots looked at the trunk of the big pine tree to see the claw marks the black bear had made during the attempts to climb the trunk. He picked up the snowshoe Migisi had thrown at the bear.

"I made the mother bear angry when I threw my snowshoe at her. I should not have done that."

Boots put his arm around Migisi.

"I am so glad to see you. I had thought the worst had happened to you. My mind told me a bear had gotten you from behind and carried you away."

"I am here, and I am hungry. I want to get back to our place so we can eat."

Boots and Migisi made good time getting back to their camp.

Over the next few days, they hunted successfully in a park near where Migisi had the encounter with the black bear. They were able to take down two deer and a moose, all without firing a shot from a rifle. Boots admired Migisi's prowess with a bow and arrow. While he managed to land a shot at a deer, it took another arrow from Migisi's bow to bring it down.

Thankful he had brought the sled to carry the bounty back to the cave, Boots tromped through the deep snow pulling hard.

Migisi tied a rope to the sled and walked beside Boots, making the pull easier.

"We took too much in our hunt," gasped Migisi. "My mother said my eyes were bigger than my stomach. I think she is right. We have enough to last through spring without all that we have on this sled."

They were two days out from their cave and Boots figured they had made it about halfway back when they stopped for the night. The tarp stretched between two trees for a covering and Migisi spread the second tarp on the ground underneath. They had found a spot protected by the trees and very little snow had reached the ground. After their evening meal, both pulled blankets to their chin for a night's sleep.

The sled that contained the hunting bounty had been pulled under the tarp and covered with a grizzly robe. The robe still carried the scent of the grizzly, and predators noted the scent and moved away, leaving the fruits of the hunt secure.

Several hours after dark set in, wolves began their haunting cry. Boots listened to the howling and he thought there were wolves on all sides of their camp.

"I believe someone else is hungry," said Migisi. "This winter has been just as hard on them as it has on everything. We have enough that we could leave behind something. It would make that howling worthwhile."

"I do not know about that, Migisi. I have never left the

meat for predators like wolves. I fear they would follow us if they know we left them something to eat."

"Well, they might follow us, but we are just one day away from our cave, and if they follow us there, we can scare them away."

The next morning, Boots watched Migisi unpack a haunch from the moose. She told Boots to not worry, there would be plenty of food to last until the snow melted, and she thought the snowmelt would come soon.

Boots and Migisi trudged on toward their home in the cave. They reached a rise that afforded them a look back at their trail, and they saw a pack of wolves fighting over the moose meat. Boots laughed, thinking there had been more fighting than eating. He counted twelve members of the pack. The leader had managed to get his fill and he lay under a tree to watch the others squabble over the meat.

After a long day of traipsing through snowbanks and pulling a sled laden with deer and moose meat, Boots and Migisi finally reached the cave. They worked quickly to get things put away before dark. Boots went to find the two horses and burro to put them back into the corral located in a park below the cave.

Migisi prepared a meal of venison stew with a recipe taught her by her father. Boots knew the aroma coming from the cave and his mouth watered in anticipation of the venison stew.

4

Boots rose early to browse around the cave to make sure nothing had been disturbed during the time they were hunting. When he went up on the hill that covered the cave, he discovered wolf tracks. The pack had followed them to the cave. Boots grew concerned about the burro in the corral. He thought the horses would be able to take care of themselves, but the burro would be the target for the wolves.

Boots followed the tracks and discovered there were only four in the pack. When they saw the pack that took advantage of the meat they left behind, there were at least a dozen wolves in that pack.

"This must be a different pack of wolves," Boots thought to himself.

He went back to the cave to have breakfast, and he talked with Migisi about finding the tracks.

"Maybe white wolf," said Migisi. "We do not see them very much. The white wolf is bigger and heavier than the grey wolf. They are to be feared because they are vicious. Two of them can take down a horse easily. They chew the back hocks to pieces and the horse cannot stand. They play around like having fun and the horse gets used to them playing. That is when they go for the back legs. There are not many of them, but if they are out there, they are hungry. You take your gun. Go find them."

Boots put together a pack to stay out for a short time. He planned to come back to the safety of the cave at night. He left early the next day wondering, "What makes her think they are white wolves. I never heard of white wolves before."

The wolf tracks showed they circled the cave and found the horses and burro. Signs in the snow showed they stalked the horses but did not attack. Boots found marks in the snow and the grass where an animal the size of a large dog had laid down on its belly. After a long search, he finally found a trail that led away from the cave.

Boots could tell the wolves had started tracking a deer. Soon, he came across the carcass of the deer. And, just as Migisi had predicted, the hock on each of the back legs of the deer had been chewed into pieces. The wolves had made a kill, and very little had been left behind. Two vultures picked at the remains.

After returning to the cave, Boots told Migisi of the find and he wanted to set up a night watch to make sure the wolves did not return to try to take down one of the horses. Migisi told him the wolves took the deer because deer were easier to pull down.

"Horses can figure things out and attack, but the deer is easier prey for the wolf. I do not think they will come back here, but we should watch, just in case."

Boots took the first four-hour watch so he could rest before leaving at daybreak to find the white wolves. Migisi woke him before sunrise and reported it had been a calm night. She had fed the horses and burro before waking Boots.

"The wolves howled last night. They sound close, but there are only four of them. We should find them and scare them away or take them down." Boots set out to see if he could trail the wolves again.

He took his rifle and six-shooter with him. Migisi decided to stay behind and make sure the animals at their cave were cared for. When she went to feed the horses and mule, she discovered the tracks were closer than she thought. She did not see any sign of the wolf during the dark, so she thought the tracks would be made since daylight.

Migisi followed the fresh tracks. Boots had followed the trail he had been on the day before. The tracks that led to the corral came from a different direction, and Boots never saw them.

The weather had warmed somewhat and the snow began the spring melt. Boots avoided areas where he would need snowshoes, and he found the wolves would move in areas where there would be little snow. He spent much of the day knowing that he tracked in circles, starting well away from the cave and working toward the home.

Migisi had found recent wolf tracks and she knew she was on the trail to find the pack. The wolves had moved to a valley that had easy access to the corral where the horses and mule stabled. The small valley had been formed with two walls coming together. Migisi moved carefully in the valley. She brought her longbow, a quiver of arrows, and she had her big knife strapped to her hip.

The pack of four white wolves found a place to rest during the day beneath a big pine tree. Migisi spotted them from about a hundred yards away. She was downwind which would make it easier for her to get close. She had made her way close enough for a shot with an arrow. The wolf closest to her lay on its side with the belly exposed.

Migisi took a step to get a firm footing as she drew back the rawhide to fire the arrow. Her step made a crunching noise in the snow and it attracted the attention of the wolves she had been stalking. The head of the wolf jolted up just as Migisi let the arrow fly. When the arrow found its target, the wolf let out a yelp. The wound would prove fatal. At the sound of the yelp, the other three wolves were up on all fours, seemingly confused about hearing the yelp. They scattered into the heavily wooded area immediately. None of the three had any concern about being stealthy as they crashed through the woods. Migisi approached the wolf she had shot to make sure the animal had died.

The wolf on the ground was a white wolf with a pelt much lighter than the gray wolf. Migisi thought the big wolf would weigh well over a hundred pounds as she set about to retrieve the pelt. The wolf was a female and she stretched out to about five feet from nose to tip of the tail.

Migisi had learned of the white wolf legends during her upbringing in her Cheyenne village. She had never encountered them until this day. She stood in appreciation of the big wolf as she drew her knife.

As she crouched and started working to remove the pelt, Migisi heard a growl, and suddenly, she was slammed to the ground over the wolf she had just killed. She managed to turn to her left side and saw another white wolf attacking. The wolf went for her throat, and Migisi pushed her right forearm into the jaws of the wolf. Her forearm landed so far back in the mouth of the wolf, the attacker could not bite down. The wolf tried to shake free, but Migisi kept a force on the forearm until she came to a sitting position.

Using her left hand, she found the knife on the ground where she had dropped it in the attack. She forced the knife into the heart of the wolf. Migisi pushed the dead wolf off her legs and stood to see if another attack would be forthcoming.

Migisi made quick work of obtaining the pelts from the

two wolves and she started back to the cave. She kept a constant watch for the other two wolves in the pack, but she did not see them. When she arrived at the cave, Migisi rolled the two pelts to dry.

Boots had spent a rather frustrating day walking in circles trying to find the pack of wolves that had an idea of taking their horse or burro. He finally gave up and trekked back to the cave. When he arrived, he saw the two bundles of wolf hides.

"Did they come up here?" Boots had a shocked look on his face. Migisi's buckskin shirt had bloodstains on the arms and chest. "What happened to you? Are you alright? Quit smiling at me and tell me what has happened."

"When you left, I went to feed the horses and I found another set of tracks. They led off to that little valley just down the mountain. I found them sleeping and I got one with an arrow. While I worked on him, another one jumped me from behind and I got him with the big knife. There are just two of them left now, and I figure they will take to the lower mountain to find something to eat."

"I do not know what I am going to do with you," Boots said as he looked at Migisi.

"What do you mean?"

"First, you get treed by a black bear and three cubs. You shoot arrows at them until they leave, then you shoot one at me while I am trying to find you. Now, while I am out searching for the white wolf, you kill one and get attacked by another."

"I am finally feeling like a Cheyenne woman. I like that feeling and I think you like it as well."

"I do like you feeling like a Cheyenne woman, but could we be just a little less dangerous about it?" Boots laughed.

5

As the days passed, the temperature stayed above the freezing mark and snow had begun the spring melt. Booming noises could be heard as the snow slides would periodically make their way down.

On the warmer days, Boots and Migisi would take their early morning coffee on the porch of the massive cave entrance.

"I am catching a hint of smoke," Boots looked to the parks below the cave.

"Yes, I can smell it, too," replied Migisi. "It is there just inside where the trees start." Migisi pointed toward a small fire just inside the tree line below. "I can see my father's brother, Harkahoma, walking this way."

Migisi stood and let out a yell to signal her uncle that he had been seen. After he returned a recognizing response,

Migisi rose from her seat and made her way to the park where Harkahoma would stop.

Boots watched as Migisi and Harkahoma talked. He could not make out any of the conversations, but Migisi began to be animated with her arms.

"Daughter of the Moon wants you," Harkahoma told Migisi. "Your son's woman is about to have a child and you must come with me. Your mother has called for you."

A year had passed since Migisi and seen her son and his wife, Ninovan. She did not know about the coming child.

"I must tell Boots. Please wait for me and I will return." Migisi turned and hurried back up to the cave. Harkahoma returned to the spot where the small fire still burned. Many braves had accompanied Harkahoma on the journey. He told them to get ready to go back to the village when he stepped into the area where they sat.

"I must go," Migisi told Boots. "Little Boots is about to become a father and I must be there. I am leaving now. You come later." Migisi did not wait for a reply as she began putting together a pack.

Boots knew there would be very little conversation about the matter, and he left to get the horse Migisi favored. By the time Boots had the horse ready, Migisi met him at the edge of the park. She quickly tied her bundle on the horse, and she swung up to mount.

"Come soon. I will be with Ninovan and her child." Migisi turned her horse and rode to meet with Harkahoma.

Fourteen braves had joined Harkahoma on the journey to fetch Migisi. An additional four braves were scouting to make sure the bunch would arrive at the Cheyenne village safely. On the last journey, Migisi and her daughter Ayashe had been taken prisoner by members of the Blackfeet tribe. When the village chief learned the two women were the daughter and granddaughter of the chief of the Cheyenne, negotiations led to their release. Extra measures had been taken to ensure the journey would not be interrupted.

Boots returned to the cave to make preparations for the trip to the Cheyenne village. The two-day journey should be easy to make with the weather being more favorable. After securing the cave Boots slept early so he could make an early departure the next day.

The horse and pack burro had not been on the trail in some months. Both seemed a bit lazy, and the burro was being more cantankerous than normal. The track to the Cheyenne village had been traveled enough that it could not be missed. On this trip, however, Boots decided on a trail that ran to the east of the track. He had been a trapper in his youth, and he had trapped beaver along the stream that wound through the forest and made its way down the mountain. He noted very little trapping had occurred during the winter. Most trappers, he remembered, would winter at the top of their run while the streams are frozen, and trap only occasionally. With the warmer weather, the trapping season had commenced, and the trappers were moving down the mountain. They would meet at the foothills in midsummer for the rendezvous.

Boots saw signs where camps had been set, but the camps had been cold for several weeks. With the warmer temperatures, Boots noticed a lot of tracks left in muddy areas. Tracks of moose, deer, elk, and bear were common. The bear tracks interested him because he wondered if it could be the same bear that treed Migisi.

6

Living in the mountains allowed the senses to become acute. Hearing and eyesight improved, but the one that improved most was the sense of smell. The nose became accustomed to the everyday smells of the trees and flowering plants, but when an unusual aroma floated through the air, the nose could pick the scent at a long distance.

Boots made his camp near the stream. He filled a pot with water and made a small fire to heat the water for coffee. A slight breeze caused him to get on the leeward side of the fire so the smoke would blow in the opposite direction. As he sat on a log waiting on the coffee, Boots noticed a hint of decay. It would not be unusual to find a carcass of an animal, and the scent picked up by Boots indicated that could be the case. Boots spent some time looking around the campsite for tracks of predators, but there were none. The horse and burro had been hobbled and had plenty to graze. They would not wander far from the camp.

He spent a restless night, hoping to reach the Cheyenne village the next day to see his family and welcome his first grandchild. Boots thought of his determination to keep his childhood family close. He had moved his mother, two sisters, and a brother to a trading post in the foothills. They eventually found themselves owning the post when the owner died. They had made many improvements, as they served the wagon trains traveling east and west. His father had abandoned the family when Boots had reached his teen years. He had become determined to break that cycle and provide his family with a father so they would not grow up without one as he did.

The small fire crackled in the brisk morning. Boots reheated the coffee left from the night before. He found the horse and burro within a few minutes and had them saddled and packed. He planned to leave after that first cup of coffee. He sipped the coffee from his tin cup as he sat on the log of a fallen tree. Again the morning breeze had picked up that telling odor, one of a decaying carcass. Boots made a vow to himself to find the source of that scent as he traveled down the mountain. After washing the coffee pot, Boots looked to the south and spotted a trail he could follow that ran close to the stream.

Once he had mounted his horse, Boots noticed the horse shied from any blowing leaf or waving branch. He patted the horse on the neck to calm him, but the more he tried, the more jittery the horse became. Boots finally decided to dismount and led the horse for some distance to see if the horse would calm.

As he walked the trail alongside the stream, Boots saw bear tracks headed in the same direction as he. When he spotted the first bear tracks, Boots stopped and studied the paw print.

"This bear must be a big one," Boots thought to himself. Claw marks measured four to six inches long and the track left a substantial dent in the muddy ground. "He is a heavy fellow, my thinking is that this has to be a grizzly."

The tracks were a few days old, but Boots became very alert to keep from having a bear encounter. He recalled Migisi climbing a tree to escape a black bear and cubs. While he could climb a tree, Boots thought he would rather avoid the bear at all costs. The bear walking on the trail appeared to be alone.

Boots walked up to a campsite where provisions were scattered over the ground. He thought perhaps the bear had found the site and decided to have a meal. Bear tracks showed up all over the campground. The fire pit contained cold ashes, and it appeared the camp had been abandoned for some time. Pots were strewn around, a saddlebag had been ripped apart and the contents scattered on the ground. The bear had eaten part of a haunch of venison and the bones were discarded near a bedroll. Boots determined there had been two men at the campsite. Both were trappers and their traps lay in disarray. The place was a mess.

His sense of smell led Boots about thirty feet into the wooded area near the camp. There he found the bodies of two men. One man lay on his belly and his back showed huge claw marks. The clothes the man wore had been ripped to shreds. When Boots looked closer, he discovered bite marks on the back of the man's neck. The other body lay on its back. Boots was startled to learn that he knew the dead man. He recognized John Ashley and he remembered him from the days of trapping in the mountains. Ashley's body had the same claw marks all over, and the same bite marks on the neck. Again, the man's clothes were in tatters.

Boots turned the other body over and learned he had found another old friend. Bill Baker and John Ashley were both on the trapping team that Boots had joined. Both were viciously killed.

The same grizzly tracks Boots had been following were around the two bodies.

Boots searched the remnants of the clothing the men wore to find some indication of how to contact family members. He remembered Ashley had family in Kentucky, and Baker's family lived in Virginia. Letters would need to be sent telling the families that the two men would not be returning home. He found the information he needed and he started digging two graves. After wrapping the bodies in their blankets, Boots finished with the graves. He paused and said a prayer over the graves of the two lost friends.

The delay had cost him precious time as he had hoped to be in the Cheyenne village before dark. However, he would have to push hard to make the village by the next morning.

After cleaning up the campsite, he bundled the provisions and stacked them at the base of a tree near the two graves. The horse and burro had been tied to the trees, so Boots mounted and led the burro down the track toward the Cheyenne village.

Before long, Boots came upon an Indian pony grazing in a small park. The rider had left a blanket on the back of the pony, and a hackamore rope dragged the ground where the pony grazed. Boots started looking for signs of the rider because he thought he recognized the maker of the blanket as being from the Cheyenne tribe. If someone happened to be alone on the trail, Boots felt as though he should at least warn the person of the possibility of a man killer grizzly. Shortly after finding the pony, he found the body of a Cheyenne brave. It was the same as with the two trappers. Vicious claw marks all over the body of the brave. Bite marks were on the neck of the young man. A bow lay nearby, the quiver had been ripped from the back of the brave, and it did not contain any arrows.

As Boots surveyed the area, he again discovered the huge tracks left by the grizzly. This made the third time the grizzly had killed a man. There are many reasons a bear might attack, but these attacks were not purposeful. The bear did not appear to be hungry, but rather powerful and raging with anger showed in the many claw marks. Blood had splattered all over the ground, indicating the bear continued the attack when the brave had gone down on the ground.

The brave had not been dead very long. Boots retrieved the pony and tied the young man to the back of the horse. He took the bow and quiver as well.

Darkness began to set in, but Boots did not want to stop until he reached the Cheyenne village. He followed the bear tracks until it became difficult to see. The bear had moved into a gulch on the east side of the mountain. Boots hoped the grizzly would stay there until he had the opportunity to return and hunt him down.

Arriving at the Cheyenne village before daylight gave Boots time to figure the best approach. He decided to tie the pack burro with the dead brave and enter with his horse. He rode to the lodge where Chief Ehane stood with several other men. After the customary greetings, Boots learned the men were about to start a search for a scout that did not return the previous day.

"I have the scout," Boots told Chief Ehane. "He was killed by a grizzly and I have brought him to you."

Upon hearing the news, the Chief and several of the younger men hurried to the area where Boots had tied up the burro. They took charge of the dead scout.

7

Boots found Migisi at the lodge where they stayed when they were in the Cheyenne village.

"I have come to see my grandson," Boots told Migisi, who laughed at the remark.

"How do you know that your grandchild is a boy? Ninovan might have wanted a girl child," Migisi grinned at the look on his face.

"Well, I guess I thought it would be a boy," said Boots as he shifted from one foot to the other. "Does not matter to me, boy or girl will be fine."

"The Great Spirit has visited Ninovan. She has both,"

"What do you mean by saying she has both?"

"Ninovan has a boy and a girl. My father, Chief Ehane says it is a sign the Great Spirit lives in this village. In all his years, he has never seen a woman give birth to two children as

Ninovan has done. We must go to the lodge of Little Boots to see the children."

Boots did not know how to think. He lived until his teen years with an older sister and a younger sister and brother. He did not have a concept of two children being born at the same time.

Little Boots stood outside his lodge talking with other young men. He had achieved some sort of status because he was now the father of two children born at the same time. When he saw his mother and father approaching, Little Boots smiled and greeted his father with a handshake, and he embraced Boots.

"My son, what has happened here?" Boots asked.

"I have a son. His name is Tahkeome, which means little robe. We will call him Little Robe. I have a girl also. Her name is Abedabun, which means the sight of day. We will call her Day."

While Boots talked with his son, Migisi stepped into the lodge to see about the health of Ninovan. She found her sitting and feeding both children. Migisi's mother, Nokomis, bustled around the lodge tending to minor details. While Ninovan had been exhausted from the ordeal, she had regained strength and smiled proudly at Migisi.

"You are better now, I see. How are the boy and girl?"

"Those two are going to be just fine," Migisi's mother interrupted. "The Great Spirit has brought them into this world and the Great Spirit will make sure they become good and brave. My grandson has done a fine thing."

Migisi looked at Ninovan and smiled, "I think Ninovan had something to do with these two being here as well."

The nursing experiences in both Migisi and Nokomis had them tending to the children and Ninovan and they did not notice Boots and his son coming into the lodge.

Ninovan held the boy up for Boots to see.

"It is Little Robe. He is going to be chief one day."

After handing the boy to Migisi, Ninovan held the girl up for Boots to see.

"This is Sight of Day. We call her Day. She will be a Cheyenne princess one day."

Ninovan's thoughts about the future were bright. It would be rare for a child born to a Cheyenne and a half breed to reach such stature, but things could happen the way Ninovan believed they would. The Chief and the village believed the two children were both brought to them by the Great Spirit so their stature had already risen to the top level.

Chief Ehane entered the lodge where everyone looked at the newest members of his tribe.

"The Great Spirit is in our village. These two children are the message from the Great Spirit that we are to take care of our young."

The chief turned to Little Boots and held out both hands.

"You must be a strong provider. You must be the strongest provider in our village because no one else has two children brought to us by the Great Spirit. You must protect Ninovan with every weapon you have for she has been the person to bring the message from the Great Spirit."

Chief Ehane began a chanting song as he sang to the newborn children. When he finished, he told the group that there would be a celebration for Tahkeome and Abedabun and he would tell everyone when that would happen. He took Boots by the arm and led him outside.

"The celebration will begin when we finish our ceremony for our scout. I thank you for bringing him to us. I must ask, did you see the battle between the brave and the grizzly? I want to know that our scout fought as a brave and gave everything he had."

"I did not see the grizzly attack him. I did notice his empty quiver, so I know the grizzly felt the fight from the scout. I can assure you that he must have fought hard."

"Sometimes it is better to not see but to know in our hearts how things happen. We will have our ceremony for the scout, after that, we will have our celebration of life for the two new members of our village, and then I want you to lead us to the man-killer grizzly. We will take all of our young braves and we will return with the robe the grizzly wears. When we find him, he will kill no more."

Chief Ehane returned to his lodge and several of the older members of the village followed him inside to plan the ceremony for the dead scout.

"I now know that our scout fought bravely against a man-killer grizzly bear. Because he fought so hard, I believe he kept the bear from attacking the men that protected my daughter on her journey here. We must have a ceremony fitting for our brave scout."

The men sat around the small fire in the Chief's lodge and smoked their pipes. The discussion about the ceremony for the dead would take hours.

Boots went to his lodge where he found his daughter Ayashe preparing food to take to the lodge of Little Boots. He rested for several hours before Migisi thought it would be time to wake him.

"My father has the village putting a new lodge together for the two children. It will be located next to his lodge and we are to decorate the outside so that it will be known that it is the home of a future chief and a princess."

"Is all that kind of thing necessary? I mean I have never been around when two children are born like this, so I have no idea about these things. They are my grandchildren, and that should be enough," said Boots.

"There is no one that has ever seen two children born at the same time. It is the reason my father is saying the Great Spirit lives in them. Even the old men and women do not know of it ever happening. So, yes, it is a big thing for this village. When word spreads, the other Cheyenne tribal chiefs will come to call on the two children and pay honor to them and my father. He will be known as Chief Ehane great grandfather to the Great Spirit children. They must live in a lodge that shows their place in our village. The lodge will be large. It will have symbols on the outside, and inside of all the things to make Little Robe and Day have an easy life. Your son, Little Boots, must provide for his family now. The old women tell me that he has done well in the village and that he cares for those who cannot hunt. They believe the Great Spirit has seen his work and this is a reward."

"I feel very proud of my son and his wife for the things they have done here in this village. I have seen a new excitement since I have come here this time. Standing right in front of me is their grandmother who fought with a black bear and her cubs," Boots smiled at Migisi. "You must take your place among these people and be careful about yourself. I followed a mankiller grizzly on my way here. A scout for you was killed by that grizzly, and I am very relieved to know that bear did not find his way to your trail traveling here."

8

True to his word, Chief Ehane called for a celebration to welcome Tahkeome and Abedabun. The weeklong festival saw dancing every evening, large feasts, and a time for paying homage to the two infants.

Migisi's brother, Red Feather, had a special relationship with Little Boots and they had become very close. They were excellent hunters and they provided much of the meat for the celebration.

"Your father and I did not get along for many years. I became angry with him when I found out he planned to take my sister away from her people," Red Feather told Little Boots. "I learned that my anger toward your father should not have happened. My father made me learn to have forgiveness in my heart. Now, here you are with Ninovan and Maheo, the

Great One, who has visited us and we have two children born at once. This is a great thing for our people and our village. Each year, my father, Ehane, has sent me as his person to the Sun Dance Ceremony. It is a ceremony where all of the Cheyenne chiefs come together to clean our arrows. Or, in your words, pray to the Great One, Maheo, for deliverance from our past deeds, and we pray that Maheo will walk with us in the days ahead. The Sun Dance Ceremony is one of the most important ceremonies of our people. My father is sending me to the villages to tell the chiefs that the Sun Dance will be held here. Each year it is held in the foothills and lasts many days. Because the Great Spirit has come to us in the manner of your two children, we will have the Sun Dance Ceremony here."

As Red Feather told Little Boots about the ceremony, Chief Ehane explained the ceremony to Boots and the elders of the village.

Most of the older men in the village knew of the Sun Dance ceremony, but since the chiefs were the only people to attend, they knew little about it. The ceremony took place each year in the warmer months. The Cheyenne know the ceremony as the largest gathering of all the tribes and to have such a ceremony at a village in the mountains would be a large undertaking. Red Feather had counseled his father to think about such a gathering a year from now. Chiefs could send people to confirm the existence of the two children. The village would have enough time to prepare to receive a large number of Cheyenne tribal members.

"We must first hunt the man-killer grizzly," said Chief Ehane. "The danger of the bear being near would not be good for our people. We must talk about the bear."

The celebration to welcome the two infants ended with the finishing of the new lodge. Little Boots had moved his family into the dwelling quietly one night to avoid the event becoming a spectacle. People in the village yearned to see the infants, and it had become difficult for Ninovan, Nakomis, and Migisi to avoid creating a stir when they took the children out during the day.

"You must go to our home and bring my things to me," Migisi whispered to Boots. "I made two bundles and I left in such a hurry, I did not remember to bring them. The bundles have things I made for the new one. In case the new one was not a boy, I also made a set for a girl. It is their clothes that I made for them. I want them now, so you must go and bring them to me."

Boots had always honored Migisi's wishes and he had begun to feel restless.

"I will leave in the morning. You know it takes two days up and two days down. It will be five days before I return."

'Yes, and if you are not here on day five, we will come for you. You must travel on the main track when you return."

Boots left in the early morning hours the next day. He took only his horse since there would be no need to put the pack burro to use. On the trip to the cave, Boots traveled on the trail near the stream that he had used to reach the Cheyenne village. He wanted to determine if there were any more signs of the killer grizzly. While he would avoid an encounter at all costs, he wanted to get an idea of the territory the bear had marked as being his territory.

No bear signs showed during the first day of travel. Boots made a small camp near the stream. Warmer temperatures with the spring weather had thawed some of the ice on the upper reaches of the stream, and the water seemed to be moving at a much quicker rate. When the blankets had been rolled out for the night, Boots could hear the mountains returning to life. A coyote yelped in the distance and a return howl soon followed. They were miles away and Boots noticed a good deal of time passed between the signals. The small fire burned brightly and a fox walked by leisurely, opposite of where Boots sipped his coffee. The fox looked to be rather lanky and in need of food. His winter months had been hard and the fox had gone without food for a long time. The fox stopped and looked at the fire and Boots, but showed disinterest when he turned and walked away.

A letter in his breast pocket pulled at Boots and he took the letter out and opened it. He turned to take advantage of the light from the fire so he could read the writing in the letter.

His mother, Mary, had penned the message and sent it to the Cheyenne village when some of the villagers had visited the trading post she operated. Boots caught up on the news from his family. He had not been to the lodge in a year, and he thought it would be time to plan a visit with his family. His thoughts ran in circles thinking of the last time he spent at the lodge. Suddenly, an air of melancholy settled around him.

Boots missed his time spent in the outdoors. He disliked having to lay up all winter because he loved feeling free out in the forest, parks, and meadows. In his younger days, Boots trapped, hunted, and fished year-round. Now, since he had aged, his mind wandered to his children and grandchildren. How the circumstances about his life had changed. Boots did not believe the mountain had changed much, but he knew the focus on important things in his life had changed a lot.

Something kept hitting the blanket and woke Boots. He did not move. His right hand held on to his six-shooter gun. He moved his eyes around trying to find the source of the disturbance. Another twig hit the blanket. Several small twigs lay in a pile on the blanket. He had picked a big pine tree for protection as he slept. Boots looked up to search the tree limbs to see what might have caused the little twigs to fall. He spotted a squirrel perched on a limb about ten feet above his head. The squirrel was chewing on something on a twig and when he finished, he dropped it. When Boots spotted the squirrel, the squirrel spotted Boots at the same time. The little fellow froze and made himself a part of the limb so he would not be seen.

Boots relaxed and smiled at the source of the annoyance.

The sun has started on its morning climb and Boots decided the little squirrel had waked him at the right time. When he threw back his blankets to get up, he saw the squirrel scramble across the branches to another tree. He stopped suddenly and turned to look at Boots. Picking up the twigs from his blanket, Boots discovered what remained of a little seedling the squirrel had been eating. Once the mystery had been solved, Boots rekindled the small fire and heated coffee. He rolled his blankets and went in search of his hobbled horse. The horse had not roamed too far and when he spotted Boots, he raised his head and gave Boots a welcoming snort.

Everything had been packed up, the horse saddled and Boots mounted to continue the second day of his homeward journey. He should arrive at the cave late in the afternoon before the sunset.

After a distance, the horse started to shy away from the trail. Boots had a hard time controlling the horse until he saw the reason the horse became jittery. A dark bundle sat in the middle of the trail. He stopped and tied the horse to a tree while he went to explore the bundle. The closer he came to the bundle in the middle of the trail, Boots realized a black bear cub lay dead.

He squatted next to the cub to see if he could determine how the cub had died. When he touched the back of the little bear, he discovered the body of the cub felt warm. He rolled the dead cub over to its left side and he noticed a little wound on the right back leg. As he looked further, Boots saw the chest and head had been mangled and there were claw marks all over the cub.

The wound on the right back leg did not look to be fresh and a tuft of hair had been pulled away from the wound.

"This must be the cub that Migisi clipped with an arrow to get the mother black bear away from the tree she had climbed to escape the big bear."

As he stood and looked at the bear cub, Boots heard a loud, fierce roar. The roar came from an area off to the right of the trail. He walked in the direction where he thought the roar originated and he heard more grunts and thrashing in the brush. Boots saw the land dropped away a few feet and in the gully, he saw the big black mother bear fighting with a huge grizzly. Boots could not believe what he saw. The black mother bear defended her cub, and the grizzly intended to kill the big black bear and the cub as well. The grizzly stood at least seven feet tall when he stood on his back legs. The big bear must weigh eight hundred pounds, Boots thought.

The fighting between the two bears could only be described as fierce. The grizzly swiped huge paws at the black bear standing just inches out of range. The black bear snarled and showed a mouthful of sharp teeth. A little cub bear had clamped its teeth on the leg of the grizzly and it shook its head with all its might.

The snarling and grunting became louder as each bear tried for an advantage. The big grizzly took a few steps toward the black bear and found the range needed for the vicious swipes of the paws to be effective. When one of the swipes connected with the shoulder of the black bear, the claws ripped open the skin and the impact knocked the bear to the ground.

When the grizzly saw an advantage to attack, he started to leap on the black bear. For protection, the black bear had the back legs and front paws up in the air and all four scored marks on the grizzly.

Boots watched the fight between the two bears with amazement. He saw the rapid movements of both bears, the survival instincts that both possessed, but he thought it would be a matter of time before the big grizzly killed the much smaller mother black bear.

Intuitively, the grizzly backed away from the bear he had knocked to the ground, giving the smaller black bear the space needed to get back up on its legs. Since the bear had been knocked down on its back, it had to roll to the side to try to stand. When the black bear rolled over, the grizzly saw its chance to end the vicious fight. Lunging at the back of the bear, the grizzly sunk it's teeth into the back of the neck of the mother bear. The strong jaws of the grizzly broke the neck of the black bear and the fight ended. The black bear went limp in defeat. The grizzly stood up to its seven feet and gave out another loud roar in victory.

The little black cub sat next to its mother who lay dying. The massive grizzly picked up the cub and threw him against the trunk of the tree where the little bear fell dead.

Boots had become awestruck at the power in the huge grizzly. It seemed as though he could pull the tallest tree out of the ground. The eight hundred pound bear had no competition in the wilds. After surveying the damage, the grizzly dropped to all fours and ambled down the slope to the gulch below.

9

With the big grizzly gone, Boots decided to skin the three bears. He dragged the cub from the trail to a spot near where the big bear lay face down. He was surprised at the weight of the little cub. His mother had cared for him well as he weighed over a hundred pounds. The cub that hit the tree was harder to move because almost every bone had been broken. Several hours passed before Boots packed the bundles of bear hides onto the back of his horse. He did not like the taste of bear meat, and he felt sure the predators would take care of the carcasses in short order.

Boots reached his home as the sun began to set. He found everything in order and he set about to make an evening meal. While he ate, he contemplated the events of the day that he had witnessed. The grizzly turned out to be the biggest bear

Boots had ever encountered. There may be more than size in the wilds, but Boots had never seen anything approaching an eight hundred pound, seven-foot-tall grizzly. The bear had killed three men and three bears and had not taken a bite out of any of them. The bear did not kill because of hunger. Boots had no way of knowing if the three men had threatened the bear and the grizzly reacted in defense. He knew the trappers well enough to think they would never try to have an encounter with a grizzly. The Cheyenne Indian scout did have a quiver empty of arrows, so there is a possibility there had been a serious encounter.

Boots had decided the huge grizzly would have to be hunted and killed. It would be a massive undertaking to keep men from being killed by the bear, but the bear must be eliminated to keep the woods and the forest safe from unwarranted attacks by the huge bear.

After a night of rest, Boots set out for the trip to the Cheyenne village. He took the main wide track as he had promised Migisi. Knowing Migisi and her concern, he fully expected to meet a contingent from the village along the track.

He did pack the two bundles Migisi had left behind in her haste to get to the village, and he had the three bundles of black bear pelts with him. The horse could smell the black bear and did not like having the smell so close. On good flat ground, a fast horse could outrun a bear. However, in the woods, a horse stood no chance of beating a bear in a race. In the woods, the bear could reach speeds close to that of the horse on flat ground and the horse would be hampered by the lack of a clear space in which to run.

Boots continued to talk softly to the horse, patting him on the neck to let him know that things would be fine. Eventually, the horse turned his attention to the forward progress and the thoughts of the bear seemed to slip to the back of its mind.

The heavily used campsite marked the halfway point in the trip to the Cheyenne village. Boots stopped for the night and found a stack of wood to start a fire. While the daytime spring temperatures continued to warm, the night air still carried a chill and the fire would be necessary to stay warm.

Boots laughed when he looked at the cold ashes. They formed a small circle inside a ring of rocks. He remembered Migisi and her lecture about the fire. Man makes a big fire and stays cold. Indian makes a small fire and stays warm. Once the blaze started heating water for coffee, Boots rummaged until he found enough wood to replenish the supply.

That had been another point in the lecture from Migisi. A small fire required a small amount of wood, and a big fire would consume a lot of wood. If man continued to build big fires, the search for wood could become difficult. Using a small amount of wood each time would allow a smaller search area for finding wood.

While he enjoyed the coffee, Boots ate a rather meager meal of hardtack and jerky. He figured he would get plenty to eat when he made it to the Cheyenne village. After the meal, he unrolled his blankets beneath a large pine tree. This time, he looked to see if any squirrels had a home in the tree. Finding no animals in the treetops, Boots settled in for a good night of sleep.

After what seemed like only minutes, Boots felt a nudge on his shoulder. He tightened the grip on his six-shooter and sprang up from his blankets. Harkahoma stepped back from the barrel of the gun pointed toward his head. When Boots woke enough to realize the source of the nudge had been Harkahoma, he put down the gun.

"My friend, you startled me from my sleep," said Boots.

"You sleep well. A bear could not wake you from your sleep," Harkahoma pointed to some tracks near where Boots had been sleeping.

Boots studied the tracks, and while the paw prints did not belong to the huge grizzly, they were very close to where he had been asleep.

"Are these fresh?" Boots asked Harkahoma. The Cheyenne Indian held the honor of being the best tracker in the village. Being the brother of Chief Ehane also put the older man in high regard.

"No, they are a day or so old. You are lucky," Harkahoma pointed to the three skins Boots packed. Boots proceeded to tell Harkahoma of the fight between the big grizzly and the mother black bear. Harkahoma had a hard time envisioning the size of the big grizzly. Boots used two sticks to mark out what he thought would represent seven feet on the ground. Boots lay on the ground with his moccasins touching one of the sticks to show Harkahoma how tall the grizzly stood.

"This grizzly is a man killer. He kills but he is not hungry. He does not eat what he kills, he kills and moves on," Boots related. Harkahoma had heard about the grizzly that had killed the scout that accompanied his party when they escorted Migisi to the village.

"I want to find this bear. I want to see this bear. I have never seen a bear this big that takes life and walks away."

"We must hunt this bear soon," said Boots as he readied his horse to continue the trip to the village. "I have a good idea where the bear stays, and I believe we can find him."

There were about fourteen young braves that accompanied Harkahoma on the trip to find Boots and escort him to the village. Boots felt very secure on the track, but he also felt the escort unnecessary.

When Boots arrived at the village, he found Migisi and Ayashe in the family lodge. They were preparing food to take to the new lodge where Little Boots and his family had moved. The bearskins were unpacked and Migisi recognized the mark on the leg of one of the cub skins as the wound she caused to get the cubs and their mother away from the tree where she had perched to get away. The two women delivered the food and then went to work to cure the hides so they could be utilized.

Chief Ehane threw back the covering to the entrance to the lodge where Boots sat next to a small fire. He had been enjoying a bowl of venison stew when the chief came inside.

"My brother Harkahoma tells me the big grizzly came to your camp and that you know where the bear stays," Chief Ehane had a stern look on his face.

"We did see tracks near my camp, but Harkahoma told me they were made a day or two before I camped. I think I can get to the place where the bear stays. I saw the bear go into a gulch near where he killed the three black bears," Boots pointed toward the three hides that had been put on stretchers to dry. Ayashe carried the hides outside the lodge and placed them one at a time against the outside wall. They would be removed and rolled up in material to soften the skin.

Chief Ehane looked at the hides and then at Boots.

"You saw the grizzly kill these bears?"

"I did watch a terrible battle. One cub had been killed when I came upon it on the trail to my home. I heard the big black bear and the grizzly having a battle near the edge that led to the gulch. He killed the second cub as he started walking to the gulch. I think that gulch is where the grizzly stays. The big bear does not eat what he kills. He just kills and walks away. He is a man killer bear."

"You rest. After three nights, the moon will be full. We will go find the bear on the morning after the full moon," the chief threw back the door covering and left the lodge.

"You are not going. I do not care what my father says. You draw a map of where you last saw that grizzly and he can follow the map. I do not want you to go," Migisi held Boots' hand. She had a pleading look on her face. This marked the first time she had asked Boots to stay behind. She knew that he would go and she would not find fault with his decision, but she wanted to make her wishes known.

Boots did not respond. He stood and stepped out of the lodge and met Little Boots as he tried to come inside. Both men stepped to the side of the lodge.

"I heard my mother say that she did not want you to go on the grizzly hunt. I know that you have to go on that hunt. The only men staying back with be the old men that cannot hunt anymore. You must go," Little Boots had his hand on his father's shoulder. "I will talk with her and I will change her mind."

"No, son. You do not need to talk with your mother about my going on the hunt for the grizzly. I will do that. You must stay here and care for your family and you do not want to get involved in matters that I can take care of. Now what kind of man would I be if I let my son try to settle my arguments? This is not even an argument. This is your mother's way of telling me what she would like to see, and I believe she spoke out of concern for me. I also believe that she knows I am going on the grizzly hunt. Cheyenne women do not tell their men what to do or not do. Your mother and I have an understanding that allows us to do what we feel is best. I know I must go on the grizzly hunt and, I will go for sure. Your mother will be happy when I return."

10

Migisi and Boots did not exchange another word about the grizzly hunt. When the sun broke through on the morning the men were to leave on the hunt, Boots found that Migisi had packed supplies and the bags were set by the door.

Boots joined a bunch of men at the edge of the village. Chief Ehane, Harkahoma, and Red Feather were at the front of the bunch, ready to head up the mountain on the wide track.

"We must head east off this track. There is a stream that runs down the mountain close to the gulch where the grizzly stays," Boots leaned over to tell Chief Ehane.

"My brother Harkahoma and I will travel with you until you find the place to turn off this track. We will go back to the village to wait for your return."

The idea pleased Boots. He also felt the thirty or forty

braves that were in the hunting party would be rather hard to manage. Every one of them would like to be the brave warrior that brought down the grizzly. Boots knew that at the sight of the huge bear, many of the braves would be in the back of the line. He had packed his rifle, a six-shooter, and plenty of ammunition. His plan would have him spot the grizzly at a distance and take the bear out with a rifle shot. The other men had brought along a big supply of arrows. One man had an old military rifle that he had found when the tribe lived in the foothills. The gun had been thrown down, it was rusted and it did not shoot well.

The brave brought the rifle along as it seemed to represent a symbol of stature for him because there were no other Cheyenne braves with a gun. The brave waved the gun in the air to rally the rest of the men in the bunch. Boots hoped the gun would not explode and wind up hurting someone when the brave fired a shot.

Traveling with such a large group meant the going would be slow. Near the end of the day, a big camp developed east of the track. Special considerations were put up for Chief Ehane. His place would be close to the fire, and there would be a wide space between his blankets and those of the others. Harkahoma and Red Feather took their spots on each side of the chief.

Boots listened to the Cheyenne talk around the campfire during the evening. All of the men were enthused to be on a hunting mission, especially one to hunt down a man killing grizzly. Chief Ehane elected several of the braves to break away from the bunch and hunt to take game back to the village.

"I know you all want to hunt the man-killer, but our village has a need for meat and there will be rewards for those who bring food to the village. It is said, and it will be done," the chief sat with his legs crossed and he looked into the eyes of every brave around the campfire. While some disappointment about not going on the grizzly hunt was felt, not a single brave showed that disappointment. Two of the men picked to hunt for the village seemed to be relieved they would not be facing the grizzly.

The next morning, Chief Ehane sent eight of the braves in different directions west of the camp. They had been selected the night before to hunt to supply the village.

"All of the braves in our village are good warriors," Chief Ehane told Harkahoma. "There are some that are very good hunters and they always help our village. The men I sent out this morning were happy to be chosen to hunt for our village. I knew they would be glad to be chosen before I picked them." The chief had a keen insight into the men in the hunting party.

Ten men left the large group and took off on their mission to hunt for the village. Boots and Red Feather were left in charge of the rest of the braves who had become anxious to get to the man-killer grizzly.

"I want to hunt alone," Boots told Red Feather. "There

are too many in this hunting party and I think somebody will wind up either hurt or dead. I think I know where the grizzly stays, and if you want to bring the rest of the hunters in behind, I would feel much easier about the hunt. Otherwise so many hunters cannot help but make noise. We will need to be close to the grizzly and attack in a surprise. We cannot outrun him in this brush." Boots pointed to the brushy gulch where he last saw the grizzly.

"Cheyenne braves are warriors," exclaimed Red Feather. "They will not follow anyone on a hunt. I must break this group up and have some of them cover the left side of the gulch, some will take to the right side and I will lead the rest down the middle. I do not know where you want to be, but that is the way the Cheyenne will hunt the man-killer."

Boots thought for some time about Red Feather's plan. He liked the idea of going in the brush in three different directions, but he felt as though the grizzly would be found on the left side of the gulch. He had spotted a trail of sorts that found its way along the rock wall on the left. He had planned to hunt along that trail.

He told Red Feather he would be in that trail, and the Cheyenne braves could hunt in the gulch any way they pleased. The men in each group needed to stay together in case they scared up the grizzly. Otherwise, the grizzly would take them out one at a time. If they stayed in a bunch, they could alert the others.

"This is not our first hunt and we know how to take down

a man killing grizzly bear. I think I wanted to know where you would be hunting so that we could hold our arrows if we see you." Red Feather turned to the braves and started to divide them into three groups. He gave them instructions on where they were to enter the gulch and proceed on each side. One group would follow him in the middle. When he turned to talk with Boots, he found him gone.

Red Feather took his hunters to the opening of the gulch. The floor spread out about four hundred feet from wall to wall. The opening stretched out to about six hundred feet. The ground cover consisted of head-high brush that grew so dense branches had to be moved to see. The group taking the left side became excited when one of their trackers found a path that contained bear paw prints. The dirt in the path had become pulverized due to the amount of traffic on the trail. Mostly, however, the tracker saw the huge paws of a big grizzly. When the tracks were first found all of the hunters gathered around to see the size of the tracks and the distance between them. They knew they were about to see the biggest grizzly they had ever encountered. The group grew quiet as they traversed the trail. Because of the confines of the brush, the braves were forced to spread out more than they felt comfortable, but the terrain could not be covered in any other manner. To make matters worse, a snow slide had dropped deadfall in the gulch and the braves had to climb over the deadfall.

11

Boots had no desire to be a hero and be the lone hunter to kill the grizzly. He felt as though the best approach would be with several men. He wanted to find the grizzly's home and gather several men to help with the attack. He found traveling the trail rather easy, but he could not see anything as he gazed out into the brushy gulch. He could hear the others trying to crash through the brush.

After what seemed like hours of trudging through the rough terrain, Boots could see the backside of the gulch and as he came near the end of the trail, he could see a cave located in the center of the wall.

When he reached the mouth of the cave, he stepped easily inside. The cave had been occupied at one time, but now it is vacant. Boots sat on a rock near the mouth of the cave and he listened to the others coming his way. Braves that had been traveling on the west side of the gulch arrived first, and those on the east side finally broke through the last of the small trees to arrive at the cave.

Red Feather and the braves he led finally crashed through the brush to find Boots and the other two groups resting at the front of the cave.

"The big bear is not here. You told me this is where he would be. Our braves could not have passed by such a large bear without knowing," Red Feather expressed his disappointment to Boots.

"I know the bear stays here. You can see the tracks everywhere. He is simply not here right now," replied Boots.

"Then we will stay here until he comes," Red Feather started giving orders to set up a campsite.

"We must leave here. We cannot stay here. It is too dangerous to try to sleep here. We should go out to the front of this gulch and get back to the stream that runs along the edge. The bear will come to the stream. It is dangerous for your braves here, Red Feather."

"Then we go now. The sun will be gone by the time we reach the front of the gulch."

The weary hunters walked to the front of the gulch using the well-worn trail on the west side. While still difficult to maneuver, the travel was much easier. Once on the trail near the stream, the group halted to rest for the night.

Boots felt some animosity coming from Red Feather, so he sat next to him at the campfire to be able to have a conversation. Red Feather spoke in a halted manner and Boots continued with his determination to find the source of the issue with Red Feather.

Finally, Red Feather began to speak his thoughts.

"We can find the big bear. My sister did not want you here because she needs you to stay with her. I know a man has to hunt, but my sister has had her say."

"I heard what Migisi had to say, Red Feather," Boots responded. "I am glad she could tell me that she wanted me to stay. But you might not know that during the night while I slept, she filled my packs with supplies and she put them next to the door when it came time to go on the hunt. She understood that I must go on this hunt with you."

Boots saw Red Feather relax his shoulders.

"That tells me my sister wanted you to stay but she knew you must go. I am better now that I know this. I know you belong here with us now."

Boots took his blankets away from the campfire where the braves continued to talk into the night. He found a spot near the stream and he unrolled his blankets as he listened to the rushing water pouring over the big rocks in the stream. The ice melt upstream caused a swift current in the stream. Boots remembered the ice melt meant the trappers on the mountain would soon be working their way down the mountain to the rendezvous. He spent many years trapping up the mountain in the fall and after the ice melt, trapping down the mountain in the spring. He had stopped trapping when the markets for beaver pelts became soft in favor of silk. He had been hunting and helping Migisi with the family in recent years in sort of a retired state.

Before sunrise the next morning, Boots woke and started rolling his blankets when a rock landed near his foot. He looked up in the tree above his head thinking maybe the squirrel had managed to find a more significant weapon to drop on him. As he gazed up in the tree, another rock bounced a foot away and hit him on the leg. Boots looked to his left and looked across the stream.

"You stay right there. I am coming over," yelled the man over the rushing water. Boots watched the man make his way to a tree that had fallen across the stream. The man stepped up on the tree and sauntered over to the bank near where Boots stood.

He saw an old man with a long gray beard. His buckskin clothing showed signs of wear. The mountain man stood over six feet and he showed to be well muscled.

He walked toward Boots and his knee-high moccasin boots looked to be a new addition. Beadwork adorned the outside of both the boots.

"If this ain't a fine howdy-do. A man I thought I would never lay eyes on for the rest of my life is sleeping across the river from my camp. I do not think you recognize your old friend Jess Raymond." Jess grabbed Boots and an embrace. He held Boots back with both hands on his shoulders. "My, but you have managed to get old on me. You were just a spring chick when I last saw you, and now here we are and you are older than me."

Boots smiled at the old man.

"I do not think it is possible to ever get older than you are my friend. I did not recognize you because you were the last person I expected to see on this mountain. I have thought of you almost every day since we parted company years ago."

"I have breakfast across the river. Come eat with me. I am alone up here and I have been worried that I might have forgotten how to talk. It will be nice to have you for company. I have been talking to myself so long that I have started believing a bunch of the malarkey that comes out of my mouth."

Both men made it across the stream by way of the fallen tree. As they ate breakfast, Boots told Jess of the man-killer grizzly that had been making his presence known near where they camped.

"I know he is out there," said Jess. "I have seen his tracks all over the place. Please do not tell me who had been killed. I am missing a couple of trappers that had broken away from our group. I'm thinking it could be them."

12

"They were trappers alright. I put their stuff beside the graves where they are buried. I thought it best to bury them where they were killed. I have sent letters to their families to let them know the two fellows will not be coming home."

"That is just a sad thing, Boots. I am sure that I want to go with you to find this big bear."

"I would welcome you, but you must know, there are a bunch of Cheyenne braves waiting for me on the other side of the stream so we can get started on the hunt. If that does not bother you, pack up and come on."

Red Feather saw Boots coming to the camp with a big rugged looking mountain man following him. When they came close, Boots introduced Jess to Red Feather.

"I think I know this man. He wears moccasins made by Cheyenne. We have hunted together," said Red Feather.

"They called me One with Sharp Knife when we hunted together. I always had the skinning duties and I could make quick work with my sharp knife. When Red Feather takes the big grizzly, maybe he will want me to skin the bear out."

Boots remembered how Jess could always make things go easier. By saying that Red Feather would be the one to get the bear, Jess became friends with all of the braves in the bunch.

"We must try to find where that bear is hiding," said Boots as he readied his pack to start the hunt.

"I have scouts looking for tracks, but they have not returned here yet," said Red Feather.

The idea to send out scouts surprised Boots because they had talked about making sure everyone had a companion on the hunt.

"I sent two on the trail by the stream. They were to go up the mountain. I sent two down the trail by the stream. They told me they saw you eating with One with Sharp Knife. They have come back, but the two that went up the mountain have not returned."

Boots frowned at the news the two scouts had not returned. The frown came from concern the two scouts may have encountered the grizzly.

"I can hear pretty good in these woods," said Jess. "I have not heard anything that would raise my hair any, but you never know. We should travel up the trail today."

Jess and Boots paired up while the rest of the hunting party spread out away from the stream.

"I have traveled down the other side of the river and I have not seen any bear signs. I am surprised he is staying on this side. There is plenty for a bear to live on the other side."

"Jess, there is a gulch further down on this side of the river, and I saw that bear go into the brush in the gulch. We have gone through there, but the grizzly had left. He is here somewhere."

Half the day had passed and nothing but paw prints that were several days old showed to the hunters. A loud Indian yell turned into a blood-curdling scream.

"I think we have found the bear," Jess tapped Boots on the shoulder and pointed in the direction of the scream.

"I think the bear has found us," said Boots. "We are going to find one dead Indian and the bear will be gone."

Two Cheyenne braves kneeled next to their fallen brother. The dead man had been mauled by the bear and the grizzly killed with the bite to the back of the neck when the man fell to the ground.

"This is one bad grizzly," said Jess.

"We are seeing the number four dead man, as far as we know."

The rest of the hunting party began arriving. Red Feather told four of the hunters to make a travois to take the man back to the Cheyenne village.

"We have not found our two scouts," said Red Feather. "Many of my hunters are finding ways to return to the village. One man left a sick woman, another wants to hunt for food, and these four men with the travois look happy to go back home."

Hunters began disappearing into the woods. Boots asked Red Feather if he thought the hunters were striking out on their own to find the man-killer grizzly.

"I do not think so. I think they are striking out for the village."

When the hunt stopped for the night, only four braves were at the camp. That left Boots, Jess, Red Feather, and four others to hunt for the grizzly. The Rocky Mountains become quiet during the dark, but tonight, the scream of a mountain lion could be heard in the distance. The lion's scream sounds somewhat like that of a woman in trouble, however, the old-timers in the woods could tell the difference. The scream kept the hunters awake for several hours.

The next day Boots learned the tracking would become even more difficult. The bear had moved into an area deep in the forest and the trees had shed pine needles and leaves during the winter making the trail even dimmer.

"What is this bear eating?" Jess asked. "I have not seen a single carcass of any animal that could have been killed by the bear. I can tell the bear is very large, and that means more food would be needed."

As Jess talked, they walked upon several bones scattered on the ground. He looked up in the trees and spotted the carcass of a deer hanging over several branches.

"Look there, Boots," Jess whispered. "That is what kept

us awake all night, and I think that lion shared with that bear. Never heard of it before, but it could happen. Maybe that bear got chased off his kill by the lion. But, I know for sure that a mountain lion put that deer up there and is roaming in these parts. That lion will be coming back for a meal."

"Bears and mountain lions do not get along. It would be a tough fight for a mountain lion to whip a bear, but it has happened. I saw a bear whip a lion years ago. That bear sat down and ate every bit of that big old cat, too," Jess remembers from his early days as a trapper.

"Do you think maybe that grizzly killed that lion and took it somewhere?" Boots asked.

"My thinking is no. If that bear killed that cat and felt hungry enough, we would see the result of that right here on the ground. The ground and the leaves do not show that a fight has taken place here. That deer up there in that tree got drug to this place by that lion. You can see the drag marks over there," Jess pointed to a little clearing where the deer had been drug through the leaves and dirt. "I think your grizzly knows that we are on his tail and he is playing with us. Everybody better be on their best behavior or risk a bear bite in the neck."

Boots could almost feel the danger in the forest. He had felt that way several times before, but this time, the feeling became much more powerful. He stopped in his tracks and looked down at the ground. When he stopped, Jess grabbed his arm.

"You are not going to turn into an old rooster chicken here are you?"

"You are crazy if you think that, Jess. Look down at the ground."

Boots had spotted the paw tracks in the dirt scattered when the deer had been drug through.

"That bear has double-backed on us and I think he is following behind somewhere."

Red Feather and the four Cheyenne hunters stepped in to look at the tracks left by the bear. Two of these men had not seen the bear tracks before and their eyes grew big when they saw the size of the tracks.

They continued following the tracks the bear left. Before long, they saw what was left of the mountain lion. The ground had been torn up in the fight between the two, and the mountain lion lost. The grizzly had feasted on the lion and blood showed signs of a struggle.

"You think maybe the lion got in a claw or two? I bet I can find a blood trail that will lead us to big boy," said Jess.

"I found it," announced Jess. "We need to bunch up here and stay together. If we stumble on this fellow, it will take all of us to put him down. I think I had rather try to paint turpentine on that big cat's rear end than have a waltz with Mister Grizzly."

Braves made quick work of retrieving the remaining portions of the mountain lion pelt and the hunting party headed north. They began to follow the tracks toward the little river and they interrupted the grizzly that had caught a meandering fox. The hunters found hiding spots behind trees. The breeze blew in their favor and the big bear did not catch their scent.

"Lawdy, I have never seen a grizzly as big as this fellow. He must stand seven feet in the air and weigh eight hundred pounds. Just look at those claws, they must be eight inches long," Jess whispered to Boots. "I sure hope this is your man-killing grizzly because if it is not, I plan to go home. This one is going to be tough to take down. If those Indians think those arrows they have will do them any good they are sadly mistaken. That bear will think it is just another tick bite if they shoot it.

"Get your guns ready. We are going to need everything we got to bring this big fellow down," Boots looked at the gun Jess held. He thought the gun to be older than Jess, but it had been well cared for. "Is that a fifty caliber?"

"It is," said Jess. "And it will blast a hole through that big tree yonder. Don't worry about this one. One of those little six-shooters you have there will be a plaything for the griz once he figures out how to shoot it"

The only sound that could be heard in the forest had to be the bear ripping the fox apart. The bear sat on his rear with his back facing the hunting party.

"I hope those boys over there will stay quiet while I figure on a plan to get this fellow. I am thinking about trying to sneak around the front and putting one of these fifties right between the eyes. I know that will mess up a nice rug when the bear has a hole blowed through its head, but I am not thinking about decorating a house right now."

"Jess, you sound like one of those wagon trains when you are in the woods. You will catch the attention of that bear before you get anywhere near a place to take a shot. If he sees you and you are alongside him and your shot misses, you will take out the other part of our hunting party over there. I think I can be a lot quieter than you if you can convince those Cheyenne to stay back, I will go around to the right and use my sharps rifle. I will not have to be as close as you with the sharps."

While this whispering discussion took place Red Feather managed to sneak up behind Jess and Boots. He tapped Jess on the shoulder and the tap almost made Jess yell out loud.

"For gosh sakes, Red Feather, I think you scared the old age right out of me. There is no way you could have come over here without me hearing you, but you did. Boots and I were just talking about circling in front of the bear and putting some lead between his eyes."

Jess looked where Boots had been standing and saw that he had left to execute his plan.

"You scared Boots plumb off. He has gone around getting in front. You are going to need to keep your hunters back and keep them quiet. I hope Boots is a good shot. If that is the case, maybe one shot, and the party is over."

Red Feather nodded his agreement and went back to

where the four braves had hidden. They had found cover behind a large tree that had fallen and all four were on the ground. Occasionally, they would peek over the top of the log to watch the back of the grizzly.

Boots had managed to move easily through the woods. He encountered a problem when he discovered there would be no place to hide once he got in front of the grizzly. It would be a chance he would have to take, plus he could get further away from the grizzly, increasing his odds of escape should something go wrong.

13

Boots found the perfect spot to step out of the edge of the woods and take the shot. When he stepped out, he would be in plain view of the grizzly bear. The shot would have to be perfect. Boots did not have any concern about placing the bullet between the eyes of the big bear. He had accomplished more difficult shots at a further distance, so he knew he could make the shot.

When he stepped out to make the shot, the bear noticed the movement immediately. Boots figured the bear would be still to try to figure the source of the movement. He brought the big gun to his shoulder. Boots took careful aim and when he exhaled, he squeezed the trigger. The loud report of the gunfire echoed through the mountains. The shot was away. Boots saw the bear dropped to all fours, however, the bear had dropped out of the trajectory of the bullet just in time to avoid getting hit between the eyes. The bullet thudded into a tree trunk behind the bear.

Boots chambered another round as he watched the bear come running on all fours. He could not believe the speed of the giant bear. He fired the second shot in such haste the shot went high. As he chambered another round, the man-killer grizzly hit boots in the chest and knocked him to the ground. The rifle flew from his hands. Boots reached for his knife which was in a sheath on his left hip. He stabbed at the bear but missed. The grizzly had not yet attacked Boots and seemed to be a little confused. He finally took a swipe and hit Boots in the head with his big paw.

Boots felt the hit and he could smell the breath of the grizzly when everything went black. He had been knocked out by the blow.

The bear started ripping at Boots' chest, leaving long claw marks from his shoulders to his belly. Suddenly, the bear jolted and fell on top of Boots crushing his chest. Boots could not breathe and he remained unconscious. The four Cheyenne braves had rushed the bear from behind to save Boots.

Jess saw the four crash into the back of the bear and he knew the weight of the bear and the four braves would probably kill Boots. He drew his tomahawk that he had carried with him since he was a boy. He ran to the front of the bear and came down hard with the tomahawk on the skull of the bear. He heard a loud crack, but the effort seemed to infuriate the bear. The grizzly started to rise and he shook off the four Indian braves. He looked straight at the source of where that blow came and roared to the top of his big lungs. Shaking his head, the grizzly started walking toward Jess.

"Good," Jess thought. "He is off Boots, but I may be taking a waltz with Mister Grizzly after all." Jess managed to get his old gun up and he fired a shot. It would be the only shot Jess could get away because it would take too long to reload the gun. Fortunately, the ball sunk into the grizzly's skull right where Jess had landed the blow with the tomahawk. The big bear weaved side to side and finally fell on its belly. Jess heard a big thud when the eight hundred-pound bear landed on the ground. He knew the man-killer grizzly would be dead.

Red Feather had kneeled beside Boots who had blood all over. Some of the claw marks were deep, but most of them were glancing blows and wound up as serious but not fatal scratches. Red Feather found Boots trying to breathe, but he did not readily regain consciousness. Jess walked over to where Boots had been knocked to the ground.

"The old gun got him, friend. The man killing-grizzly is no more," Jess did not know if Boots could understand what he said. "Red Feather, I need to check his chest to see if he has anything in there broken."

While Boots had not breathed any frothy blood as an indicator of broken ribs, Jess felt along both sides.

"I do not know how he did it, but I do not think any of his

ribs are broken," said Jess. Broken ribs that punctured a lung meant sure death in the mountains.

It took the Indians several hours to procure the skin of the man-killer grizzly. They also obtained the claws from all four appendages. They looked in awe at the huge claws. They wanted to move away from the site where the bear lay. Nobody wanted any bear meat, and the carcass would be left to the wolves and coyotes.

Taking care not to injure Boots anymore than he had already been hurt, they managed to place him on a travois and move him to an area where they could camp. Long strips of sinew had been attacked to the front of the travois and it had been made long enough so that two men could put the pull strap on their heads and make the pull. There were six men and each team of two would take a turn. Jess tended to Boots during the night. He told Red Feather that he wanted to stop by his old camp to get his pack because he had plenty of cloth to wrap the gouges on Boots' chest. One of the braves had made a poultice to smear on the wounds, but they needed to be cleaned. Jess said he could take care of that when they reached the stream.

The travel went very slowly as those pulling the travois tried to avoid the areas where elevation changes would cause problems.

Late in the day, they reached the area where they had camped when Jess joined them. He crossed the stream by walking on the fallen tree and he returned with two large packs. Jess had left the few beaver hides that he had harvested. He thought the trappers coming down for rendezvous would pick them up. He hauled water from the stream using a cooking pot and a pot that he used to boil water for coffee. He put the filled pots on the coals of the fire to boil out any impurities in the water. After the water had cooled, Jess took strips of an old shirt and washed the blood and the wounds on Boots' chest and his head. Jess had found where Boots' head had landed on a rock when he fell and a big gash had been bleeding. Once the wounds had been cleansed, the poultice was once again smeared on and Jess wrapped clean cloth around Boots' torso.

"We must hurry him to our village. My sister, Migisi, is a healer and she can make him well again," said Red Feather.

"I remember Migisi and I know if we let anything happen to him we had better run fast and far because her vengeance would be severe," replied Jess.

As the hunters started to get tired more frequently, Jess took on more responsibility for pulling the travois. Jess stood much taller and he had more power in his legs. The last few miles in the journey, Jess did all of the pulling. When they finally reached the village, Red Feather directed him to the lodge where Boots and his family were staying. After freeing Boots from the travois, Jess carried him inside the lodge and put him in a bed that had been hastily prepared. Migisi did not talk very much as she cared for Boots.

14

After getting Boots settled in his lodge and Migisi taking over his care, Jess stepped outside to survey the Cheyenne village. He had not visited this village before and he was surprised that Boots had a lodge for his family. A young woman walked up to Jess and introduced herself as being Ayashe.

"It is very good to meet you, Ayashe. I hope I said that right. Sometimes I am not very good with names. My name is Jess Raymond."

"Yes, you said my name right. It means Little One. I am the daughter of Boots and Migisi and sister to Little Boots."

"So this is where his family lives," Jess raised his eyebrows in surprise. He did not know Boots had children.

"My father and mother live in a cave high up on the mountain. They came here because the Great Spirit came to visit Little Boots and his woman Ninovan. Because the Great

Spirit came, Ninovan had two children at once. She gave us a boy and a girl on the same night. The boy is Tahkeome or Little Robe, and the girl is Abedabun, or Sight of Day. We will call her Day. Migisi's father, my grandfather, says the Great One has brought us these children and we are to have the Sun Dance here next year."

Jess knew of the Sun Dance ceremony and he knew the ceremony is the highest in the Cheyenne culture. To host the Sun Dance Ceremony would be a high honor bestowed only on Cheyenne royalty. He also knew that twin children did not happen in the Indian world so this is indeed a rare event.

While Jess and Ayashe were talking, a man walked between the two and turned to Jess.

"You are the man that kept the man-killer grizzly from taking the life of my daughter's man. My name is Chief Ehane, and we shall have a celebration to mark the death of the man-killer and we will all come together to try to help Boots return to us as we knew him. I will have a place of honor next to me for the man who saved the life of the man named Boots."

"I am told by my uncle Red Feather that you saved the life of my father. I am glad to meet you. If you are Jess Raymond, my father talked of you often. He taught me many things and said, 'This is the way Jess would do it and I finally get to meet the man who did so many things. My name is Little Boots."

Jess reached out his right hand and Little Boots met the hand for a handshake.

"Yes, I am Jess Raymond, but I do not think I did all the things your father said I did unless they were all good things. If they were good, then I did them all," Jess laughed.

"Yes, they were good things. I am glad you are the one that saved his life because now we have one more thing to say "This is the way Jess did it," Little Boots and Jess both laughed.

Chief Ehane stepped back into the conversation.

"I heard Ayashe tell you of the visit from the Great One. They stay in this lodge, and you must come to see what the Great One left us."

The chief pointed to an elaborately decorated lodge. Braves were milling around near the opening to the lodge and they stepped aside when Chief Ehane, Jess, Little Boots, and Ayashe came to enter.

Two older women were helping a younger woman with the two children. Jess took in the expanse of the lodge thinking it to be very large, unlike any other lodge he had seen.

Little Boots stood beside Jess and he leaned over to speak softly.

"Little Robe has been named chief, and Day has been named princess already by Chief Ehane. Their place in the tribe will be confirmed next year during the Sun Dance ceremony. I am the father and I hardly get to touch them before I am shooed away by those women," Little Boots grinned at Jess.

"It is probably just as well, son. A man has no business around the raising of children until they reach the age to go hunting. That is when the man takes over from the women," Jess grinned.

Chief Ehane left the lodge and made arrangements for Jess to have a place to sleep and a place where he could put his packs. When Jess stepped outside the lodge, a young man took him to his quarters where Jess found a nice lodge, and when he went inside a small fire had been lit and a woman started cooking food.

"This setup could be just right for old Jess Raymond." He found the right spot for his packs and removed his blankets to spread on the soft bed of leaves and pine boughs. Jess sighed as he lay back. He covered his eyes with his forearm, and before long sleep had overtaken him.

The woman cooking the meal for Jess woke him with a shake of his shoulder.

"You get up now. You sleep all the time. Food is ready and you eat."

The shoulder shakes startled Jess and he overreacted by sitting up quickly with his knife in his hand.

"You do not need a big knife to eat," the woman laughed at Jess. She turned away and found a place to sit away from the fire.

After Jess got his bearings, he sat with his legs crossed and spooned some of the stew into a bowl. He found the stew to be delicious and he nodded to the woman to come to join him. She shook her head no. He felt a little uneasy with someone watching him eat, but he did eat because he had not eaten in a day or so. She kept telling Jess, 'plenty more' and he would get another bowl. When he finished, he told the woman thanks for cooking and he left the lodge with his stomach bulging from so many bowls of stew.

"Did Plenty More fix you with some good food?" Ayashe asked. She came out of the lodge where Boots lived.

"That is her name? Plenty More? I thought she wanted me to eat more, she kept saying Plenty More and I kept getting another bowl of stew. I am a big man, but I have never eaten so much in my life," Jess exclaimed.

"Yes, her name is Plenty More," laughed Ayashe. "Her man died years ago, and there is no one left that can help her since her son started his own family. She is a good woman."

"I know a good cook when I see one, and she is a good cook. I will try to provide for her while I am here," Jess said. "How is Boots coming along?"

"He is not awake. My father has a fever now and is talking out of his head. We are trying to keep bathing him in cool water. My mother is hoping the fever will leave him soon because it has been with him a long time."

Jess made a motion toward the lodge and Ayashe grabbed his arm.

"It is not good for you to see him yet. He has no clothes

and mother is working to keep him cool. Sometimes he shakes and she has to cover him quickly. I will tell you when you should see him."

Jess picked up two buckets and told Ayashe he would get water from the stream for Migisi. Ayashe nodded her head in approval.

Chief Ehane called all the village members together around a big bonfire in the middle lane of the village. He told everyone that the celebration had been called to mark the death of the man-killer grizzly and to honor the men that brought the grizzly hide to the village. Ehane recognized Red Feather and the four hunters that were with him. He also talked about Boots and his brave attempt to kill the bear. Finally, Ehane introduced Jess Raymond to the people and told of his effort to kill the bear and save Boots from certain death.

The bear hide had been spread out on the ground before the chief. People were surprised at the size of the bear. Ehane held up two necklaces to show the size of the bear claws that came from the grizzly. One necklace held the claws of the front paws and the other necklace had been made of the claws from the back feet.

"There are two men who should wear these to show their bravery. One will be given to Boots when he recovers and the other will be given to the man who killed the grizzly and saved the life of Boots.

Ehane placed the necklace with the claws from the back

feet of the bear around Jess' neck. The claws were huge. These types of necklaces were normally worn by braves with high standing in the community. Jess had earned just such a standing. When it came time to enjoy the feast, Ehane took Jess by the arm and showed him the seat of honor being next to the chief on the pelt of the man-killer grizzly. Drums picked up the celebration beat and the braves began their dance. The drums, the Indian hoots, and hollering became very loud.

"We will watch until we eat. They will dance while we eat. It will be a long joyous night for us," Chief Ehane spoke loudly in Jess' ear so he could be heard above the noise.

'I wish my friend Boots could be with us to take part in this celebration. He is the one who found the old griz and figured a way to kill it. If it had not been for Boots, we would not be celebrating."

"I wish it also, but I know my daughter will have him healed as soon as she can. Her mother is helping her and she is also a healer."

Chief Ehane began to sway with the rhythm of the drums and the dancers. He sat with his legs crossed on the hide of the big bear.

It looked as though the dancing would go on through the night. When one set of braves tired from the dance, another set stood ready to take their place. The young women would dance to spell the braves. Jess began to feel the efforts of the day.

"I think I must go find my blankets, Chief. This has been a great celebration and I am glad your village had this to enjoy. I must bid you good night."

"It has been a long day, Jess. I know that Plenty More will take care of everything in your lodge. Have a good sleep."

When Jess went inside the lodge that had been designated for him, he saw that Plenty More had placed her blankets next to his.

"What is this?" Jess pointed to the blankets.

"My name is Plenty More. I am honored to be at your service. You are very important here and I will cook for you and make your clothes. You must come to your blankets because your eyes are very tired."

Plenty More rubbed Jess's temples after he lay on his blankets and within minutes he fell asleep.

The celebration continued into the early morning, and many of the revelers decided to continue after a brief rest. Chief Ehane had left the festivities well into the night. He had left instructions to tell everyone the festival will continue after sunrise.

Jess woke with the rhythm of the drums, and a call of "Ho,Yo,Ho,Ho,Yo" in song. He could hear the bells strapped to the ankles of the dancers, and many of them carried sticks hollowed out and filled with small rocks. Those sticks served as a noisemaker and they were shaken in rhythm with the drums.

He looked over to find Plenty More gone from her blankets. Some breakfast food had been set on a flat rock near where he slept.

15

Sometime during the night, Migisi thought the fever had finally left and Boots started resting more comfortably. She had changed the bandages on his wounds and paid special attention to the gash on the back of his head. A white cloth circled his head to keep the gash from bleeding.

Ayashe had fashioned a partition to hold blankets. The enclosure helped block the noise of the celebration. She had also begun to make Boots new buckskins. His shirt had been ripped to shreds and his pants were so bloody they would never be worn.

Jess put his head through the opening of the lodge.

"Would it be alright if I came in to see Boots?"

"Yes, you can come. But, you must know he is in a deep sleep and will not know you are here," said Migisi.

"That is alright by me. I would just like to sit with him a bit so you can do other things."

Migisi welcomed the relief and handed Jess a wet cloth.

"His fever has left, but I try to keep this on his head to keep him cool. He may get chills, so just cover him if he starts shaking. I am ready for him to wake up."

"I think this whole village is ready to see old Boots take a trot out of here. He missed a party in his honor last night."

"I heard every bit of it," Migisi held up the bear claw necklace.

Jess went behind the partition and sat on the ground next to Boots.

"I am beginning to think you are milking this thing a little too long. You have all these women in here taking care of your every need, and here you are acting like you are sound asleep. I come a long way in my years, and I do not recall ever having to sleep so long."

Jess thought he saw an eye partially open.

"I know you can hear me. I am of a mind to go out there and tell Migisi that you are just pulling her leg with this and she needs to take a switch to you to get you out of bed."

Jess tried to get some liquid in the patient's mouth. He held Boots up a little and tilted the cup so the tea could go in his mouth. Boots seemed to drink the tea, and before he knew it, Jess saw the cup empty. He gently lay Boots down.

"I bet if that cup held some old whiskey you would be up to dance a jig. Speaking of dancing, you are missing a big party out there. I ate more than I can eat last night and watched so much dancing I thought I might have a try. Now can you just imagine seeing this old mountain man's beard flopping around out there?

Jess kept up the conversation with Boots. He reached over and took Boots' left hand in his.

"I know this is a tough thing to come back from, but you are going to make it. I sure would like for you to let me know you are coming back. All you have to do is squeeze my hand a bit. Do not go and try to break it, just a little squeeze will get me by."

Jess felt a light squeeze from Boots and his eyes lit up.

"I thank you for the little note there partner. We are staying with you until you come out of this and I hope that is soon. That woman, Plenty More is a good cook and she is going to fatten me up like an old fat turkey if I am not careful. I am getting Migisi back in here, and you better be nice to her or you will have me to answer to."

Jess stood and went into the main part of the lodge to find Migisi with tears in her eyes. He sat beside her.

"Now listen here. I want you to know that Boots is close to pulling out of this thing because of your help. I can tell these things. We are going to have to be ready when he gets better to make sure he can walk and all that stuff. It is close to being good news back there."

Migisi had wiped away the tears and she looked at Jess.

"You are a good man. You saved Boots from the bear and

you brought him to me. Boots has talked about you in the past and I know he counts you as his only friend."

"Well, if the things he said about me were good things, then I did every single one of them probably twice. If they were bad things, I did not do any of that stuff."

Migisi laughed at Jess's comment. She stood and went to sit beside Boots. Jess stayed in the lodge for a while and finally went out to watch the ceremonial dancers. Chief Ehane saw him leave the lodge and ask him about Boots.

"I know he will be awake soon and he is going to be ready to go hunting in a short time." Jess smiled at the chief.

Boots continued to mend. One day when Jess stepped into the lodge, Migisi asked him to help Boots into a sitting position so he could eat comfortably. The request surprised Jess because the last time he saw Boots the man did not have a conscious bone in his body. When he stepped around the partition, he saw that Boots had opened his eyes. When Boots saw Jess, he put a frown on his face.

"I do not know why you frown every time you see me. You need to quit doing that. Are you are going to start messing with my head about it someday?"

Boots chuckled and started to laugh, but the chuckle turned into a moan when pain shot across his chest from the sore ribs.

"I am in here to help you sit up so you can take some food. If I can get you to stay still long enough, I will get some stuff that Plenty More has cooked and you will soon be as good as a new saddle. Yep, just a little stiff, but ready to ride."

Jess lifted Boots so Migisi could pack some things behind him so he could lean back but still be sitting up. Boots moaned at the pain caused by the movement. Jess wondered if Boots had fully regained his senses because he had not spoken.

Migisi nodded her thanks to Jess when he said he would be back with some of Plenty More's stew. Plenty More would not hear of Jess taking the stew to feed Boots.

"I will take my stew and I will make sure he can eat it. I know you would just put it in his mouth without watching. I want him to enjoy the first food he has had in a long time."

Jess had learned that Plenty More had her ways about her, and he had become accustomed to her ways. He even had come to like the way Plenty More conducted herself. Jess had decided that he and Plenty More would be a good match for each other. A cantankerous old mountain man meets a Cheyenne woman with plenty of wisdom and experience to challenge that mountain man.

As she spoon-fed Boots, she kept repeating Plenty More when the food went down his throat.

"I have to warn you Boots. I heard that plenty of times until I ate myself sick. Her saying Plenty More does not mean you need to eat Plenty More, it means she is telling you her name. Look out at how much of that stew you eat." Plenty More shooed Jess away from Boots and she kept feeding him.

Migisi enjoyed the exchange between Plenty More and Jess.

"I know that my Boots can tell Plenty More when he has had enough. It has been many days since he has eaten though and he does not want to eat too much." Migisi went to help Plenty More feed Boots.

When Jess left the lodge, he encountered Chief Ehane.

"How is our man Boots coming along?"

"I do not rightly know for sure. One minute I think he is ready to pull out of it and the next, I think he likes all the attention those women are giving him. He has had so many baths he is starting to smell like lilacs and roses. They are in there right now fussing over how much food he needs to eat to regain his strength. He is sitting up, but he is not talking."

"I will see him and I will try to edge him toward talking. When he starts talking, Boots will be up and walking soon." The chief entered the lodge and witnessed the women fussing about trying to keep Boots comfortable.

"I know you feel like you must make him feel good about being where he is, but sometimes a brave needs a little prick to remind him that things must be done, that he has a lot of life to live, and that life cannot be lived on those blankets. I will talk to him."

Chief Ehane walked around the partition. Chief Ehane talked low to Boots and Migisi could not understand what her father told Boots.

Chief Ehane started putting his hands on Boots in various

places asking him if he felt pain. He told Boots to nod yes or no for an answer. After the chief checked several areas with Boots saying there had been no pain, he put his hands around the throat.

"Do you feel pain where my hands are resting?"

Boots shook his head no.

Chief Ehane put his hands down.

"Since you do not feel pain there, I am telling you it is time for you to talk. You do not have to say anything aloud, whisper to me your name."

"My name is Boots and I am ready to be healed," whispered Boots.

"This is very good young man," the chief replied softly. "I will return later and we shall talk more."

The chief did not say anything to anyone as he left the lodge.

Red Feather invited Jess to take part in a hunting party that would last for several days. Jess agreed to go saying he had started to get lodge fever staying indoors all of the time.

About twenty hunters went on the expedition and every time a game animal had been taken, two of the hunters were to return to the village with the carcass. Jess watched as the Cheyenne braves took down many deer and antelope. Jess believed he had seen a pronghorn dashing across an open area. The pronghorn is among the fastest on four legs and he challenged the braves to see if they could take the pronghorn.

Red Feather asked Jess if they were good to eat.

"I have never been able to take one down to see how tasty they are," answered Jess. "Today would be a good day to find an answer to that question."

All of the braves in the hunting party had an opportunity at the pronghorn, but unfortunately, their arrows fell to the ground while the pronghorn skipped away. Red Feather had noticed the pronghorn did not seem to be bothered by the many arrows that came his way. He simply outran the shot.

When the pronghorn had been sited again, it came to Red Feather to take his turn. He stepped to the front of the group as the pronghorn grazed. A snap of a twig alerted the animal of danger. When he raised his head to find the source of the noise, Red Feather gave out a whistle.

The pronghorn turned toward the area where he thought the whistle originated. In the time it took to spot the source of the whistle, Red Feather had loaded his arrow and fired. As he unleashed the arrow, Red Feather whistled a second time. Being startled by the second whistle, the pronghorn did not run and the arrow found the mark just behind the shoulder. The pronghorn fell to the ground with an arrow in its heart.

"We shall taste the meat tonight," Red Feather turned and smiled at Jess who stood with his mouth open. "Sometimes it does not matter how fast you are when someone smarter is stalking."

The braves cut a haunch from the pronghorn and two hunters took the rest back to the village where folks stared at the unusual-looking animal.

As the hunt continued, Jess could hear other hunters whistling to freeze a running animal. The hunt became very successful and as night fell, they had an opportunity to taste the pronghorn.

"I know why this fellow has to be so fast. If everybody knew how good this is, they would drop everything else and hunt only him."

"There are not many of these on this mountain," said Red Feather. "I can count the number and we are eating one of them now."

Early the next morning the hunting party came to an area where Red Feather knew plenty of deer and elk stayed. They would linger in the woods and step out into a nearby park to graze. A little wet weather creek ran nearby for water.

Red Feather laid out a plan for the hunters to circle behind the game in the woods. They were to set a line of flames to move the game toward the park where they would hurry and be ready to shoot when the game stepped out of the woods.

"This is our way of taking food back to many people in our village," Red Feather explained to Jess. "We must be smarter than the food we hunt."

Jess had seen places where a fire had moved to a park much in the same manner. He had thought the fires had been started by lightning strikes. He had no idea of this hunting method Red Feather described.

Some of the hunting party left the camp before daylight

to circle behind the game and they intended to set the fires. Jess, Red Feather, and the rest of the hunters went to the park to find a place to set up a skirmish line so they would be ready when the game came out of the woods.

Jess noticed smoke coming through the tops of the trees about a half-mile from the park. It did not take long for those hunters who set the fires to join the rest of the hunting party. They were set in a perfect spot. They faced the breeze and that breeze would push the fire toward the park and the game would be coming out soon. He could hear the crackling of the fire and occasionally a dead tree would make a loud noise when it fell and hit the ground.

Hunters did not have long to wait before the first bunch of deer came running out of the woods to escape the fire. The deer turned toward the wet weather creek to get water. When they turned, arrows flew through the air and found their targets. The hunters were firing arrows as fast as they could get loaded.

Jess did not shoot. He did not feel his bullets would be of any more help than what the hunters were bringing down.

Suddenly, a big moose came lumbering through the woods. Jeff sighted in his gun as the moose crashed through the trees. He followed the moose into the park and fired as he cleared the edge of the forest. The moose went down and a deer trailing behind had to make a big leap over the dead moose. Red Feather let an arrow fly as the deer reached the peak of the leap and the deer fell dead within inches of the moose.

By the time the flames died out, hunters were in the park processing the deer. Deer carcasses littered the park. Jess stood next to Red Feather.

"Why are all the hunters laughing and pointing to me?" Jess asked.

"This is the end of the hunt. We have to take back what we took today. My braves settled for little deer. Good enough to feed people, but not so heavy they could take back three or four at a time. You took the big moose. That moose weighs more than ten deer and you are going to have to pull it to the village. It will feed a lot of people, but the moose is old. The meat will be hard to chew. But, you were able to get the old slow-moving moose, so you get to take it home," Red Feather grinned at Jess.

"Harrumph," mumbled Jess. "My eyes are bigger than my brain. I guess I had better get to work."

All of the hunters made a lightweight travois each to haul their game back to the village. Jess had to make a travois using heavy limbs to haul the heavy moose.

As the hunters started to the village, they managed to get on the wide track that would provide little resistance to the travois. Jess lagged behind, and every once in a while, one of the hunters would drop back to relieve him so he could take a breather by pulling one of the lighter-loaded travois.

Jess trudged along the track pulling the heavy travois. He

kept thinking the hunt did not take place this far from the village. He used his head to pull for a distance, then he would switch to his arms. Jess had experience pulling sleds of beaver pelt bundles, but they were nowhere near as heavy as a moose.

When the hunters finally arrived, Jess pulled the big moose to the area where the women were processing the meat. One old woman pointed to Jess and indicated he should haul the moose to another area. She shook her head at Jess and the moose. When he finally dropped the travois, Plenty Moore showed up with skinning knives.

"Man shoots big moose and we starve. Hunters shoot little deer and we eat. On the next hunt, bring little deer," Plenty More continued to mutter as she fell to skinning the moose and processing the meat.

Jess sneaked to his lodge and fell to his blankets and promptly went to sleep.

16

After the conversation with Chief Ehane, Boots began a swift healing process. He would have scars on his chest, but the wounds had healed completely. The gash on the back of his head had healed and the lump where his head hit a rock had gone down. Boots had regained consciousness, but he had difficulty talking. He became flustered when the words he tried to speak did not come out the way he wanted them.

Migisi worked with him so he could relearn how to talk. He fared better in the Cheyenne language and that flustered him even more. If he could do things using the Cheyenne language, why could he not make his language work properly?

Boots did not want Jess to see him in such a state, and Migisi had done everything she could to convince Jess that Boots had not healed enough to see him. Jess knew that he had healed. Standing outside the lodge near where Boots had his bed, Jess could hear Boots trying to learn to talk. The difficulty talking did not matter to Jess at all, but he could not convince Migisi of that. Jess talked fluent Cheyenne. He told Migisi that he would speak the Cheyenne language to Boots if she would let him in to see him. The pleas from Jess did not work. He had a feeling that Boots did not want to see him until he could talk plainly like he did before the battle with the grizzly.

Jess got the bright idea one morning to stand behind the lodge next to where Boots had his bed. He would carry on a conversation and maybe he could spark Boots into letting him in the lodge.

Jess started the conversation using the Cheyenne language. It so happened Chief Ehane came by, and Jess grabbed him by the arm to stay with him and talk.

"Well, Chief Ehane, it looks like my days here are numbered," Jess said in a loud voice. "I know, I know, you want me to stay here forever, but I must move on. You think you have found a place where you might stay for a while, then the old mountain starts working on you and you figure you have to move on. I am thinking about heading on up the mountain. I hear there is a cave up there where a man could settle down and raise a family. Me and old Plenty More could go up there and spend the rest of our days in that cave and be happy."

Chief Ehane did not have any idea about this conversation, so he did not know what to say to Jess. Jess kept pointing to his ear and then pointing to the lodge, but Chief Ehane did not understand.

"I am going to roll up that hide from the man-killer grizzly, get some supplies for our packs and we will be heading out soon."

Chief Ehane had mixed emotions about Plenty More leaving the village. He knew she needed someone like Jess to protect her and provide for her, but he did not think she would be up for such a long journey."

Jess kept talking and rambling on about how wonderful it would be to live in a big cave. "A feller could hunt when he wanted, shoot, the winter weather could be tolerated in a cave like that. I think it is probably a good place for me and Plenty More to go." Jess continued hoping that Boots heard what he said and would have some sort of reaction to it.

Before long, Migisi came out of the lodge and walked to the back where the chief and Jess stood. She shot daggers at Jess and took him by the arm to lead him to the front of the lodge.

"You get in there. He wants to talk," Migisi felt anger about what she had heard and hoped that Boots could talk Jess out of going to their home.

"You grey, bearded old man, I am not plowed under yet. I will make it to that cave before you and I will happily kick your rear end out of there if you think you are going to homestead my place," Boots talked in his language. He looked surprised that he could string all those words together without faltering.

Jess grinned at Boots and offered his right hand.

Boots looked a little confused, but he met the gesture with his right hand.

"Welcome back to us partner. I do not have any plans of homesteading your place. I wanted to stir your juices enough to get you to come out of that stupor you have been in. I think it is time for you and me to take a stroll out of this place. I know you can walk. I have seen through the walls you walking around in here."

Jess reached both hands out and helped Boots to his feet. Boots wore moccasins and new buckskin clothes. Jess put Boots' left hand through his arm and he held the hand there with his left hand. When they walked around the partition, they met Migisi.

"Mam, we are going to take a stroll and we shall return shortly. We'll be ready for some of your delicious stew when we get back."

When the two men stepped out of the lodge into the sunshine, Boots winced. He had not seen daylight in such a long time that it took a few minutes for his eyes to adjust. Chief Ehane stood on the other side of him beaming with a big smile.

Jess and Boots took a stroll down the midway of the village. Those sitting outside their lodge used their rattles to signify their enthusiasm for Boots.

Migisi had prepared a meal for the two men when they returned to the lodge. As they sat to eat, Boots began to talk.

"I think I would like to go to the trading post and see my family," said Boots while he looked at Migisi. "We have not been there in a long time now, how long has it been?"

"Little Boots went with us and he had not married, so yes, it has been a long time," Migisi replied.

"Where is this trading post you talk about?" asked Jess.

"The post used to belong to Trapper Kelly. I took my mother, two sisters, and a brother to live there after my father abandoned them at the farm. My mother married Trapper Kelly. He died a few years back and now my family operates the post. My brother has set up a blacksmith shop to take care of the needs of the wagon trains passing through east and west."

"I remember Trapper Kelly's place. We would stop there for supplies when we finished with the rendezvous and we headed back up the mountain. I did not know that was your family."

"I do remember Trapper Kelly had a lady and her daughters helping. The trappers would find reasons to go in there just to see those girls," Jess laughed. "I would kind of like to travel along with you. I have not been to the foothills yet this season. I have no business there, but old Jess is getting a little weary lately. It might be time I struck out for a place now. I wonder if Plenty More would like to go along. Of course, she would be there only to cook and stuff."

"It is a two-day journey to the trading post," Migisi said. "We usually take a cold meal to eat along the way, but if you want to come along and bring Plenty More, I am sure the folks at the trading post would like to meet you."

The three talked about making the trip over the next few days. They would be riding on the way, and there were questions as to whether Boots could ride. He and Jess slipped away early one morning and saddled two horses. Jess helped Boots get mounted in the saddle and he rode alongside to give Boots enough confidence that he would not be worried about slipping off the back of the horse. Several days of riding and Boots finally found his old riding habits coming back to him. When his head hit that rock, the impact must have jostled his mind and after a while, things started coming back.

The day before they planned to leave, Jess stopped by the lodge to tell Boots and Migisi some news. He had a jubilant look on his face when he entered.

"I have talked with Plenty More about going along with us to the trading post. It seems as though she has never left this village and she wants to see the rest of the world. So, that means she will be coming along. I have bought her a horse and she says she knows how to ride. I even talked with her about me settling down somewhere. She is not so sure about that, but she said she would take a look at it."

The reason for the happy look on Jess's face became apparent when he spoke those words.

Jess helped Boots load the packs on the horses and all four

were mounted and ready to leave the Cheyenne village. Boots sported the bear claw necklace given him by Chief Ehane. That necklace marked the end of the man-killer grizzly adventure.

Migisi rode beside Plenty More and they talked about what they would see on the journey.

"When we get to the trading post, you will meet the family. Mary, Julie, and August are the family. I think June has married and moved away, but June and August are still there. Mary is Boots' mother. She is a kind woman and takes good care of her family."

Plenty More took in all of the scenery. She had been out scouting around the village on her own, but she had never ventured very far.

With Jess riding by his side, Boots began to feel a little closed in.

"When do you think you are going to learn that I can ride a horse without your help? You are hovering over me like a mother bear over her cubs. Well, I guess that probably did not come out the right way. But, anyway," figuring he had already said enough, Boots quit talking.

"Now you have started something you cannot finish. Me hovering like a mother bear over her cubs? Well, I saw a man-killing griz hovering over old Boots and for a while there I thought that bear was whispering in your ear asking you for the next waltz. Of course, you would probably have agreed to it if you had not been knocked out cold by that rock. You know it took all four of those Indian hunters and me and Red Feather to roll that dead grizzly off of you. And we sure figured you for a goner once we got him off, too. That feller used those claws on you and it is a good thing you fell on your back. I think if you had fallen any other way that old grizzly would have chomped down on your neck like he had those other men and you would have been under a stack of rocks right now instead of riding beside one of the best and prettiest friend you have ever laid eyes on."

"I am not so sure about the prettiest part, but I am for durn sure about the best friend part. I guess if you have to hover it will be alright by me.

Boots and Migisi knew the trail to the trading post well enough that they continued riding through the night. The horses did not seem to tire since they were traveling at a walk.

"What is the first thing you are going to do when we get to the post, young man?"

"I am going to give my mother a hug and then sit down to a big breakfast with my brother and sister. You can come along with me too as long as you do not go hugging on my mother. You, Migisi, and Plenty More will all be welcome at my mother's table."

17

Mary, Julie, and August were about to sit at the table for a breakfast meal when they heard a rider stop at the front porch of the trading post.

"I wonder who that could be at this hour of the morning," Mary said.

August stood and walked through the post and unlocked the front door. When he stepped out on the porch, he saw Boots and Migisi, along with Jess and Plenty More.

"Well, look who has come to see us," exclaimed August.

"Who is it, August?" asked Mary.

"It is my brother Boots along with Migisi and two other people. It looks like they traveled all night to get to see us, too. Y'all get off those horses and get in here for some breakfast. Young Lizzie will be by here and tend to your horses. She runs our livery down yonder." August pointed to a big barn with a large corral."

Boots led the way as they all went into the trading post. After giving Mary and June a hug, he turned to August and shook his hand.

"It is good to see you again brother. Things are looking good here so I know you have been taking care of things."

Plenty More could not believe her eyes as she surveyed the merchandise in the trading post. Blankets were stacked on shelves. Strings of different color beads hung from the ceiling in one corner, giving the place a festive look. Bolts of cloth were laid out so the patterns could be easily seen. Plenty had never seen so many things she cherished in such a large number in one place.

Jess stepped to her side and held her hand. He began to explain to her how the trading post worked and that people came in to either trade for goods or to pay money for them. He doubted that she heard much of what he said because she had been so taken with all of the products in the store. He turned to the group and introduced Plenty to everyone after Boots had told them the big ugly mountain man happened to be his best friend Jess Raymond.

"Come everyone, have a seat, and let us enjoy breakfast," announced Mary.

Jess eased over to Migisi and spoke softly to her.

"I am sure you can understand if we take our breakfast outside and eat. I am pretty sure Plenty More has never eaten at a table before and I think she would rather not eat if she had to sit and let everybody watch her."

"You two go on outside. There is a place you can eat around the corner of the building. If you want to build a little fire in the pit, that will be fine too. I will bring your breakfast to you."

Jess nodded his approval and he eased Plenty out the front door and they walked around the corner of the building to find a perfect spot to have breakfast. Jess started a small fire in the pit and Migisi brought out two plates heaped with bacon, ham and biscuits, and gravy.

"I think this food will be enough, but if you need more, just let me know and I will take care of it. Do not worry about what this family is thinking. They are used to this. Boots and I ate out here a lot before I got the nerve to try eating at a table."

August and Boots opened up a storage building behind the trading post and they pulled out several tarps and a big tent. They set the tent up and laid the tarps on the ground as a barrier between the damp ground and the bedrolls.

August asked Jess if he and Plenty would like to sleep in the tent and Boots and Migisi would sleep outside.

"No, we will sleep outside, but I want to run a rope between those two trees and we will stake out one of the tarps for shelter in case of rain. We will be fine that way."

The rope got strung and one of the bigger tarps laid over

it. When the tarp got staked to the ground it allowed enough room for two people.

"Boots and I have lived in this tent for a long time," Migisi told Plenty.

"We are not going to sleep right now, are we? Breakfast took only a few minutes," said Plenty.

"No, we want to get things set up and we will walk about and look at all the new things that have been put here since our last time here."

"Boots, I think I remember you saying something about a blacksmith shop here. Am I right about that?"

"Yes, August built the blacksmith shop with the help of a master blacksmith. He studied under the blacksmith long enough to become a master. He handles just about anything the wagon trains need. You will find a Charter Oak wagon around here. That wagon belongs to the doctor and his family. August went to the factory where they build those wagons, and he and the doctor have put together some nice rolling stock."

"There is a doctor here?"

"Yes, Ike and his wife Betsy and daughter Lizzie were coming through headed back east because they had enough of California. They stopped here for a while and decided to stay. Their house is across the road from the trading post. I am sure you will be seeing them soon. Ike has been a big help here. Two fellows tried to rob the store and one of them hit mother over the head. She was knocked out for several days and the doc took care of her."

"That sounds like something you might have gotten from your mother because you did the same thing when that old griz laid atop of you," laughed Jess. "You probably should get that doctor to give you a look over to make sure we got things taken care of the in the right way."

Jess and Boots started walking toward the big building that housed the blacksmith shop and the stables. Jess could hear the hammer clanking against metal.

"I guess I never told you that I have heated a forge a few times in my early days. I started to be a blacksmith. I did pretty good with it until the mountains started calling my name. I sold my business and used the money to stake me in my journey to the Rocky Mountains. It is kind of funny that after I lived my dreams for so many years, I come back to that hammering noise and I like it. He is hammering out a horseshoe. I can tell by the way he starts and stops and the sound of that hammer."

When they walked into the front door, August doused a horseshoe in a bucket of water to cool. He pulled it out and then put it back in the forge for heat.

When it turned red hot, he pulled it out and began hammering again until he had it the way he wanted. The hot horseshoe went back into the bucket of water again. After a short time, it cooled enough for August to take another look. This time he liked what he saw and called Lizzie to bring a horse into a stall. He looked up from his work and saw Boots and Jess watching.

"How are you fellows doing? I am about to shoe a horse if you want to watch."

"We will be fine, August. Jess here used to blacksmith in his younger days. Where is your helper, George?"

"George fancied a lady on one of the wagon trains and he hitched a ride with her to go west. I have been short-handed ever since and I have had to turn business away because I could not get to it. Oh, well, that is the life I guess."

August took four horseshoes with him when he went to the stables.

"Jess, if you are thinking about staying, I bet August would give you a tryout. It sounds like he could use the help."

"It sure would be something to do if I decide to stick around."

They walked around to the back of the building where the corrals held several horses. A young lady sat atop a bay horse and she gave the horse exercise around the corral. She stopped in front of Boots and Jess.

"Hi, Boots. If you two are looking for something to do, I am about to take these horses to the river for a swim. It sure goes a lot easier if I have a little help."

Plenty and Migisi had walked up and leaned their arms on a corral post.

"These two lazy old coots would not be any help, but

Plenty and I will be glad to ride to the river with you. We will not need a saddle so we can just walk right in."

"That would be great, Migisi. I usually get to take a bath when I take the horses, so I have plenty of soap."

Lizzie put bridles on two horses and the trio soon had the bunch of horses headed for the river.

August met Boots and Jess as they walked into the shop.

"I am having trouble getting this shoe to fit that horse. Would you mind taking a look and maybe helping me get this shoe straight?" August looked at Jess. They walked to the stable and Jess picked up the front leg of the horse to study the hoof in question.

"This hoof has not been trimmed right and it has grown out of round kind of. Hand me that shoe."

August handed Jess the shoe. He placed the shoe against the hoof and studied the correction that would have to be made to the shoe so it would fit the hoof.

"I think I can fix it. It has been a long time, and I usually do not make it a habit to use another man's furnace. But, if you are willing, I will give it a try."

August motioned with his arm for Jess to go ahead.

Jess heated the shoe and hammered it a bit, then drenched it in the water bucket. He looked at it and went back to the furnace. He drenched the shoe several times before he became satisfied the shoe would fit.

"That is a tough one there young man. If this shoe fits, I would advise you to not sell that horse until we have that hoof corrected. This shoe will work for a while, but it will need to be replaced."

August took the shoe and placed it on the hoof of the horse. The fit could not have been more perfect. August finished the shoeing by nailing the shoe in place.

"I thought that horse had lamed up when he got here. I did not pay much for him, but he never got over that limp. I can see why now with that hoof being the way it is. Do you think we can get it fixed?"

"I am sure we can. It will take some time because you do not want to take too much off there in one whack. A fellow will have to shave it off a little at a time."

Jess turned around to say something to Boots, but Boots had left.

"I see my sidekick has gone off and left me here. What else can I help you with so you can get caught up?"

After talking things over for a bit, both men set to work clearing the backlog off the storyboard hanging on the shop wall.

Before long, the bunch of horses started filing into the corral. Lizzie, Plenty, and Migisi were not far behind. All three women were talking and laughing.

"It will be three days before I take the horses to the river again. I sure hope you two can stay around to help. I had a lot of fun."

"We enjoyed the swim ourselves. We all smell like lilac

and roses now and that should give Boots and Jess a pause," they all laughed at Migisi's remark.

They met Betsy and Ike when they returned to the trading post. Betsy helped Mary and Julie in the store. Ike liked woodworking and building things. It did not take long for all of them to get along.

Later that evening, Jess and Plenty took their food to the spot next to the wall of the trading post. They talked about the day and the enjoyment they both experienced.

"I have been snorting that lilac and rose stuff you have been wearing. What is that stuff, anyway?"

"It is in the soap we used when we took the horses to the river. We were able to swim and bathe. It probably would not hurt you to go down to that river and get wet every once in a while."

"I might do that very thing, but I am not taking that lilac and rose stuff when I do go." Jess laughed. "I like it just fine on a woman, but there would be a problem if a man had that stuff on."

"Plenty, I have a hankering to stick around this outfit for a long time. I am kind of hoping that you might want to stick around here with me. Oh, we could go back to the village every once in a while so you could see your family. You are kind of growing on me, and I am hoping that I might be growing on you just a little."

"I do not know about this growing on people stuff, but I

would like to stay around with you for a while, especially if you say we can go back to the village when we want to."

"I think we can do that. I am going to help August in the blacksmith shop, and I bet Mary can find plenty of things for you to do around the store. I know you make some really good buckskin clothes and I saw only one set in there. They could use some more. We can talk with her tomorrow and get that lined out."

"I think this old good-looking mountain man has found a place he would kind of like to root around in for a while. I know this is going to be hard to believe, but Plenty has decided I am not so bad after all, and she wants to hang around with me for a while, too. I am looking to see if we might be able to get that tent of yours when you decide to go back home. We could make a good home in there." Jess told Boots.

They were sitting on the front porch of the trading post having this conversation when Ike walked up.

"Did I hear somebody say they are going to start living here?"

"I believe that Jess and Plenty have decided they want to put some roots down here. Jess is going to help August in the blacksmith shop."

"I will start felling some trees today. Let us go pick out a good spot for your cabin," Ike motioned to Jess to follow him.

"While I am doing this, could you talk to Mary about

Plenty helping out some? She will need something to do and she can make good buckskin clothes."

Boots agreed to talk with Mary and he watched Ike and Jess traipse off to the woods.

"Plenty has never lived in a cabin before. I am pretty sure she will get used to having a different kind of roof over her head."

"There is one thing about it, Jess. If she gets tired of it, she can always find a place to sleep outside."

It did not take long to find the ideal spot for a cabin, and Jess started hearing the ring of the ax as Ike started taking down trees to make a cabin.

"Mother says welcome to the neighborhood, Jess. And she told me that yes Plenty would be a big help making buckskin clothes. They have had to buy the clothes and have them shipped here. It will be a relief to have someone that can make them here."

After doc pronounced Boots fit as a fiddle, he and Migisi loaded up to head to the cave in the mountains.

Jess and Plenty watched Ike build their cabin. They were looking forward to settling at Trapper Kelly's trading post.